This is a work of fiction. Similarities to real people, places, or events are entirely coincidental.

IT'S NEVER TOO LATE

First edition. June 5, 2024.

Copyright © 2024 Catherine Sans-Souci.

ISBN: 979-8227860644

Written by Catherine Sans-Souci.

IT'S NEVER TOO LATE

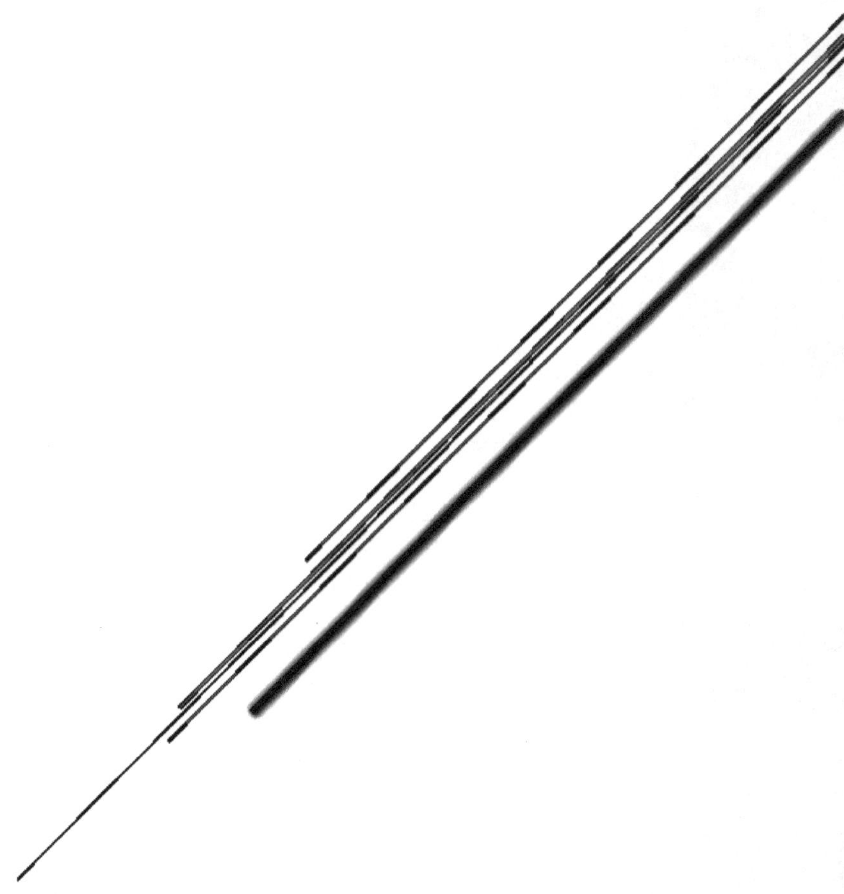

Catherine Sans-Souci

Dedication

I dedicate this story to:

- Mireille, who was like a real mother to me for over forty years.
- My mother and father, with whom I have made peace.
- All my ancestors.

I love you.

A big thank-you to my friend Maude for coaxing this story out of me.

A heartfelt thank you to my friend Julie for expertly editing the text.

Introduction

A good friend of mine, one I hold dear, recently confided in me that she is having trouble walking away from her second toxic marriage. She wants to leave her husband, and has been talking to a therapist, her children, her siblings, friends. We are all in her corner, but she still has cold feet about leaving. Why?

It's not as if there is anything to salvage from the marriage. She and her husband haven't had a pleasant conversation in years. Why is my friend hesitating to walk away from someone who clearly doesn't love her? Why, given the reality of her situation, does she still have doubts?

I ask why, but it's a rhetorical question; I know what she's going through because I've been there. Not so long ago, I was my friend. I know all about the doubts, the second-guessing, the guilt, the shame, the anguish, the despair, the broken-heartedness, the futility, and sheer exhaustion of it all.

My conversations with my friend brought back those days when I, like her, would continually find reasons to stay in a marriage where I wasn't loved.

A few days ago, she left her husband and shared with me how relieved she was. I was so happy for her. Inspired by my friend's strength and, in honor of the person I am today, I decided to write the story that follows.

It's the story of a woman born in Haiti in the early fifties, but who lives most of her life in the Unites States. By the time she reaches middle-age, she is overcome by the uncertainties of life but transforms herself to become a strong, carefree, child-like, serene, creative, and, at times, fearless person.

I have come to believe that where and when we are born may not be simply an accident of fate, and that we ourselves may have a hand in it. So, why would the woman in the story have chosen to be born in Haiti?

In my view, Haiti is a place with a strong potential for negative energy; it's prone to catastrophic earthquakes, it's directly in the path of recurring devastating hurricanes, its past history rests on the most horrific of human experiences - brutal slavery; and its recent history is one of chronic self-serving politicians and rampant criminality.

Everywhere on Earth, life is difficult; it's the nature of the place. In Haiti life is particularly difficult. For those born there, the pull to live one's life in the negative is strong.

Early childhood is a determining phase of a person's development; hers was branded by the energy of Haiti and became the foundation on which she built her life. I believe that she chose to be born in Haiti to test her resolve to live constructively during her time on earth. As the story will show, it was easier said than done; the testing was considerable.

Haiti's saving grace is its enormous resilience and creativity. Its people are the most wonderful artists. Creativity and the capacity to endure are very powerful energies, and the woman in the story chooses to tap into them to develop her life.

In some areas she had no difficulties. She had no trouble differentiating right and wrong. Fighting off temptations like smoking, drinking, taking drugs, stealing or cheating came easily to her. Where she fell short was in self-confidence, taking responsibility for what she hated about her life, and finding the strength to choose joy over fear.

It took years for her to understand how a toxic relationship can undermine one's self-confidence; to understand the human tragedy that comes with thinking it's all right to live with a partner who doesn't love you.

None of what she achieved came easily. She had to work relentlessly for each gain. But in the end, she takes charge of her life and learns, step by step, how to change. She trusts herself and, while she delights in her friendships, she doesn't "need" someone else to make her happy.

Life is good.

Chapter 1: Haiti

My name is Marie-Chérie Blémot. Family and friends call me Chérie. When I was small, they called me Ti-Chérie.

I was born in Port-au-Prince, the capital of Haiti, at a time when commerce was flourishing and the island was a popular tourist destination; when the hills were covered with lush vegetation; when even the poorest ate every day; when the academic standards of the state university were high; and when a young woman like my mother could aspire to a doctoral degree and dream of building a good life. I came from an upper middle-class family and, seen from the outside, I lacked nothing and enjoyed a charmed childhood.

My memories of Port-au-Prince date back to the early sixties. I was eight when I left Haiti, so my experience of the city was limited by my age and a life that revolved around family activities and school.

What I recall is a bustling, congested city. Even in those days the downtown streets were crowded and noisy - vehicles tooting their horns endlessly, people talking animatedly and mobile street vendors loudly advertising, in their unique sing-song way, the merchandise they carried on their heads.

I loved the food vendors. My favourites sold pastry and *fresco*, a treat made of shaved ice. The *fresko* vendors pushed a wheeled cart decorated in flashy colours typical of the tropics; it contained a large slab of ice wrapped in thick canvas. They used a hand-held metal device which shaved, compacted and moulded the ice. They then drenched it with tasty syrup. Given the heat and the lack of a container, you had to eat the *fresko* very quickly and your mouth would freeze in the process. I would gladly have lived off those *fresko*.

In the midst of all this intense activity, competing for space with vehicles and pedestrians were the vendors on donkeys and the barrow pullers. In my memory, all the donkey-riding vendors were women. It was quite a sight to see these women riding side-saddle, carving their way through the commotion. "Assertive" doesn't begin to describe the panache with which they expertly handled their mounts and sliced their way through the throng, sometimes against traffic.

If I found the donkey riders entertaining, I was borderline scared of the barrow pullers because of the extreme effort they had to exert to move their loads; their faces were etched with tension. They hauled huge two-wheel barrows (probably originally designed to be pulled by an animal) to take mountains of goods around the city. They transported everything from crates of chickens to machinery, fuel, large sacks of rice; whatever people needed was moved by the barrow pullers.

It was literally scary to watch them go—they were constantly a hair away from a fatal accident—their loads were so heavy they couldn't stop abruptly if needed. Also, once they got it moving, they didn't want to lose their momentum so they forged ahead no matter what.

Despite the overwhelming chaos, the experience was thrilling; it was full of life.

The residential neighbourhoods where my parents and close relatives lived were charming, with quiet streets. Most of the properties were walled-in, typical of the islands, so you could only get a glimpse of the beautiful houses with their bright, well-kept gardens through the grilled gate. The yards were spacious, with mature trees to provide shade and a constant cool breeze. No two houses were alike.

On weekends we spent the day at the beach. I loved the sea. On Sunday afternoons the classic outing of a middle-class family was a stroll along the *Bi-centenaire*, a lovely esplanade built along the bay of Port-au-Prince, featuring majestic palm trees and a beautiful, illuminated water fountain.

My happiest experience of Haiti was the *defile kanaval*—the carnival parade. Carnival is a mega-event in Port-au-Prince that draws people from all walks of life into a three-day celebration culminating on Mardi Gras (Fat Tuesday). The whole population is literally overcome by celebration frenzy. People pour into streets and are swept away by the carnival spirit. We watched the *defile* from a second-floor window at a friend's house that afforded a perfect view.

In my memory, *defile kanaval* was magical: gorgeously decorated floats, the best local bands, performances by fabulously costumed dancers and extravagantly dressed paraders. The procession moved along the main streets of the city to the contagious rhythms of *konpa* and *rasin*—two of the most popular music genres in those days.

The colours of the costumes alone were enough to dazzle the eyes. "Delirious" is way-too-tame a word to describe the fever-pitch excitement. People didn't just dance—they ecstatically abandoned body and soul to the music. Their bodies flowed with jubilation, energy, passion, and fervour. I have never experienced anywhere else such intense elation, such ardour for the celebration of life.

In Haiti my father was in the construction business. He owned and operated a cottage factory that manufactured coloured cement tiles, very popular in the Caribbean, and he did terrazzo flooring. He was known and appreciated for the artistry of his tiles. The original colour combinations and patterns in his tiles and the designs he integrated into his terrazzo flooring set him apart. He was very much in demand and his business flourished.

My father couldn't suffer drab, lifeless people. He loved life and appreciated creative spirits. So, to build my character he did not treat me like a fragile little princess; in fact, he mostly treated me like a boy and introduced me to his work when I was still quite young.

Around him I was always perfectly behaved and focused. If he told me not to touch a machine at the tile shop, I understood and never disobeyed. By the age of six I was so familiar with the operations of the shop that I knew how each piece of equipment functioned, how to mix cement and colour pigments, and could have shown anyone, step by step, how to mix, mould and decorate the perfect cement tile. I also had strong opinions regarding colour combinations and patterns for decorating the tiles.

Often, after hours, my father would bring my mother and me to the construction site where he was working to show us his current project. My sister was there as well but she was still a baby. These visits are by far my happiest memories of family life. My father would go on and on about colour choice and pattern while my mother and I listened adoringly.

If there is one thing my mother loved about my father it was his creativity. To include me in the conversation during those visits, my father would take the time to ask me simple questions such as whether I liked his choice of colours.

Although my father died too early to know that I became an architect, it was he who put me on the path to that career choice. I remember being as young as four when he would pick me up and draw my attention to the line of a building which he considered beautiful, or to a streetscape which he found harmonious. While I was sucking my thumb, my little untrained eyes would try to zero in on what he was pointing at. He taught me to appreciate the beauty of cities.

From my mother I inherited the drive to work hard and the desire for a good career. She taught me about discipline and perseverance. I remember as if it were yesterday the day she came home with her doctoral degree. Her pride that day was almost palpable; she glowed. Her pleasure and satisfaction had such a positive impact on me that I decided on the spot that I wanted to experience that kind of success one day. I also recall thinking that only hard work would get me there.

Unfortunately, the peaceful and comfortable days of Haiti were not to last. The first signs of political tension came with the curfews. No one was allowed in the streets after dark.

Being young and hard-headed, my father sometimes acted irresponsibly and would come home from a construction site after curfew. When it happened, my mother would be out of her mind with worry and she would give him quite the scolding when he finally arrived.

I remember that this was when adults began whispering about the political situation in the country. Everywhere you went, the atmosphere was very strained. I didn't know the meaning of the word "insecurity", but I certainly knew what it felt like.

My accident was another example of how things were changing in Haiti. Our neighbourhood was in the suburbs. My school was in the city. Every day in the morning, my father drove me to school. After school a helper would pick me up and walk me to my aunt's nearby house. Later in the afternoon a hired taxi would take me home.

One day, when I had almost reached my aunt's house, I saw her husband pulling into the driveway. I loved that uncle; he and my aunt spoiled me to death. It was unusual for him to come home from work that early in the day. I was so excited to see him that I slipped from the hand of my helper, dashed across the street without looking and was hit by a car. I fainted on the spot.

My aunt was later told that while passers-by and neighbours came to my rescue, the driver of the car that had hit me took off without giving me a second glance. Clearly, he had no qualms about leaving a child he might very well have killed lying on the pavement.

Fortunately for me, I survived. But this type of reckless and reprehensible conduct was becoming the norm; it exemplified how the fabric of our society was disintegrating.

Chapter 2: My Branding

Although I was very young, I knew of our president, the infamous figure *Papa Doc*[1], and his *Tonton Macoute,* paramilitary secret police known for their brutality, terrorism and assassinations. The horrors described by adults penetrated my world, making me aware of violence and injustice, at the age of six.

One day when I was seven, that violence and injustice touched my family directly, shattering our world and altering the course of our lives forever. My father was arrested and taken to prison because, as we later learned, he had insisted on being paid for a construction job he had completed. The customer didn't see it that way and decided to show my father who was in charge.

Fortunately, someone who knew my father alerted my mother to his arrest. With the help of family, she moved heaven and earth; my father was released that night. Although detained for just one day, he had been badly beaten and needed immediate medical attention.

When he arrived home the following day, I didn't recognise him. He couldn't even stand up. Gone was the handsome prince whom I adored and had, when I was four, pledged with all my heart to marry when I grew up. His eyes, usually soft and full of humour, were now filled with terror.

While he was sitting and being tended by my mother, our gaze connected briefly; life stood still and I felt the full measure of his despair. It left me breathless. The experience was traumatic, and left me paralysed with helplessness, a feeling I was already familiar with.

Fear and panic saturated the house. In the following hours and days, I made myself small and kept out of the adults' way. In the span of a few hours, our lives were wrecked and my childhood ended as I learned a hard lesson - that from one minute to the next, life can rob you of everything.

About a year later my mother and I left Haiti on a *Pan Am* flight to New York City. It was almost nine months before my father and little sister joined us. Except for the cash my parents were able to put together without attracting too much attention, and what they carried in their small suitcases, they left all their possessions behind. Our circumstances were not unique; hordes of Haitians fled, as we did, to escape a bloody dictatorship and the criminality it engendered.

Seeing my beaten father was not my first traumatic experience. From the age of six I was sexually abused by three men who worked in our home. I didn't tell my parents. Even at that age, I knew that talking about it would only make things worse. My father loved me; if he learned about it, he would go into an uncontrollable rage and would have the men beaten to a pulp. Physical violence is a way of life in Haiti. Even at six years old I understood enough to know that I didn't want this violence on my conscience.

My mother was a difficult person and didn't love me. I knew that if I told her, she'd accuse me of dropping a "filthy situation" in her lap, and would have deeply resented me for it.

One adult of the household was aware of what was happening to me: Marthe.

Our beautiful house had two wings on either side of a rectangular central area with common living room and dining room. Each wing had two bedrooms, an office and a bathroom. A generous porch ran across the front and back of the house. At the back, beyond the garden, there were broken-down maid's quarters.

My parents shared the house with two adults; a brother Albert and his sister, Marthe, whom they considered family. The brother and sister occupied one wing of the house and my parents lived in the other with me and my sister. The adults respected one another's privacy and met only in the common areas of the house. My sister and I visited the other side when we were invited by Marthe or her brother.

My parents moved into that house because their financial situation was improving and the neighbourhood was a step up. Sharing the house made it more affordable – at least that's what my parents believed at the time. Years later, after they had left Haiti and Marthe's brother had died, my parents learned from the owner that the monthly rent they paid, which was supposed to be half of the total was, in fact, the full amount. The whole time we lived there they were scalped by people they considered family.

Marthe knew from day one what the male help were doing to me. She chose to scold me in a tone filled with disgust, and told me I was a "dirty girl" who liked *anba vant gason* - literally "below the belly of men." She made me feel ashamed, and certain that it was my fault.

In every instance, when one of the men arrived to work Marthe called my little sister to her bedroom and closed the door in my face. This behavior convinced me that I was to blame for what was happening. Much later in life I realized that probably all it took was a menacing look from the older man to tell Marthe that if she blabbed, there would be consequences.

If my understanding is accurate, she understood and feared the older man's meaning and gave the three men the space they needed by shutting herself in her room for a long time. Because she liked my sister, she took her to protect her. If anything came to light, she could always hide behind the excuse that she "didn't see or hear anything" .... To protect herself, Marthe threw me to the wolves without a backward glance. And I offered no resistance. Every time one of the men gestured for me to follow, I complied.

The men never approached me when my parents were home; only when my parents left my sister and me with Marthe. Summer holidays were the worst. I tried to escape, begging my mother to stay with my aunt but sometimes she said no, and accused me of not wanting to play with my little sister. When she didn't allow me to go to my aunt's, I was fair game. I would have lived permanently at my aunt's house if I could have.

Many years later, when I was in my fifties, I realized that my mother must have been aware of the sexual abuse I endured. How, over a two-year period, could she, not even once, have noticed my soiled clothes?

I experienced stress at school as well. Haiti's education system relied on abuse; physical punishment combined with humiliating verbal punishment. My mother didn't allow the nuns to beat me; however, verbal abuse was permitted and I got plenty of it. Every morning I had stress-related stomach cramps before going to school in Port-au-Prince.

At the age of six, I had lost all innocence: I had learned to rely only on myself and to bottle up everything inside. I had a very low opinion of myself. During those years, I developed severe rashes on my fingers and palms, as well as chronic conjunctivitis. The hand rashes diminished when I left Haiti. The conjunctivitis lasted until I was forty. Even today, stress can give me stomach cramps and hand rash.

Chapter 3: Adapting to Our New Life

Because the political situation in Haiti was becoming more threatening and dangerous, many people wanted to leave the country. But they had to do so discreetly; typically, families split up to escape, taking minimal belongings. My mother and I left the first; my father and my sister followed later.

The only way I can describe my shock upon arriving in New York City is that landing on Mars could not have been more difficult. Everything around me was foreign- the sounds, the smells, the buildings- there was glass everywhere- people's appearance, the language and the pace of Big City life.

Alien card holders entering the United States for the first time had to show a clean bill of health. The day we flew to New York my mother carried the required X-rays as well as test results and proof of vaccinations.

The doctor who examined our documents at the airport expressed concern about an alleged spot in my mother's chest X-ray. We were therefore not allowed to enter the city and were immediately quarantined and taken directly, under guard, to the Staten Island Hospital. My mother was not allowed to speak with the relatives who had come to pick us up. They were notified of our situation by an immigration officer.

The hospital was a huge complex which had a number of "inside" rooms, like the one we were given, where the only window looked out on an air shaft. We seemed to be encased inside a dark and very deep well.

A loud, but undefinable mechanical hum characterized my experience of the place. I didn't know at the time, but it was simply the sound of the city. We spent two days at the hospital and I vomited constantly during our stay. I wasn't sick; I was simply overwhelmed by tension because there was nothing in my surroundings that I could relate to. Even the water tasted foul.

When hospital doctors confirmed that my mother was in good health, our relatives came to take us to their home. Their warm contact and loving support helped us adapt.

A few weeks later we settled even more when my mother found an apartment and sent me to school. Not speaking a word of English was a challenge, but the hardest part of school was managing lunch. The cafeteria was located in a gloomy basement and I had never been in a basement before. A few nuns were responsible for serving the food which consisted of half a sandwich, a small bowl of heated canned soup, a small carton of milk and a small bowl of dessert.

I didn't have to speak English to understand that I had to get in line like the others, pick up a tray and find a spot at the table where my classmates were sitting. My problem was what was on my plate. It didn't look like food to me or smell like food either—trust me, baloney and mustard between two slices of day-old bread is an acquired taste.

The tomato soup tasted too sweet and too acid. I had never drunk pure milk before- in the Caribbean we don't guzzle milk like people do in North America. So, I tried the dessert. That at least I recognised as a fruit, but I almost went into convulsions when I tasted it. When your only experience of fruit is intense sweetness, the bitterness of American canned grapefruit is enough to make you gag, which I did, of course.

The lunch experience was horrible. Because I was new, the nuns were indulgent and didn't force me to eat on the first day, despite the hard rule that students had to finish the contents of their tray. I didn't need any translation to grasp that either. They distributed my lunch amongst the children sitting around me.

From that day onward, however, I furtively gave my food to the other children. I became very popular when hot dogs were on the menu. During the months I spent at that school I never ate a single bite at lunch.

Another shock was snow. We lived in Manhattan and my school was about four long city blocks away from my home. That's a very long walk for a child, particularly one like me who, before coming to New York, had never walked on the street alone.

In Haiti, it would have been unthinkable to let me walk home from school alone. In New York there was no transition, I had to become self-sufficient overnight and walk to and from school by myself every day. After school I was alone in the apartment until my mother arrived from work at around seven p.m.

On the first day, my mother took a day off to walk me to and from school, but after that I was on my own. Because all the tall buildings looked the same to me, to avoid getting lost my mother pointed out a few landmarks at my eye level to help me get my bearings. So, I made mental notes of things like the bakery at the corner of our street.

One day it began to snow early in the afternoon. My school was U-shaped and our classroom was inside the U, on the fourth floor. I noticed a change in the colour of the light outside, the sky became drab and it began to snow large, fluffy flakes- an absolutely enchanting sight seen from the classroom window. But when I left school a few hours later, I was stunned when I stepped outside.

The school had no yard and the front door of the building was aligned with the edge of the sidewalk. The moment I stepped outside I was lost, so much so that I had to press my back to the wall of the school to cope with the vertigo that assailed me.

People who have seen snow since they were born are not really aware of how much snow transforms scenery. They can recognise what their winter neighbourhood looks like from past experience. I did not have this reference. That I was in this new place, so far from the home I knew and remembered, and had no sense of where to even begin finding my way home was overwhelming.

The snow had stuck to the façades of all the buildings, covered the vehicles parked along the street and blanketed the sidewalk. The streetscape had changed so drastically, it was as if someone had played a trick and changed the street scenery, as they do for plays. Other than the building I was leaning against, there wasn't a single recognisable feature that I could use as reference point- I totally lost my bearings.

A force inside me held me tightly until the panic subsided a little. The force told me not to look at my surroundings and to think this through. So, I looked down, and in my mind, walked my way back home. I knew that coming out of the school I had to turn right, go to the first street light, cross the street, turn right again and walk until I reached the intersection of my street. To fight the vertigo, the force told me to keep my eyes cast down and follow my mental map.

The force reminded me that, on my way to school that morning, the window of the bakery at the corner of my street had been full of beautifully decorated cakes and I had admired them. So, on my way back that afternoon, I told myself to look for the cakes in the window to know when I had reached my street.

After walking what was clearly way too long, I realised I must have passed my street- I had walked too far and had to turn back and start over.

Focus, said the force.

I think I missed the bakery twice. Finally, I stopped and I told myself to pay close attention to every single display window.

Good girl, approved the force.

In the end, I found the bakery. I hadn't recognised it because I was looking for the cakes. By this time of the day, they had all been sold and the display window was empty. Despite my difficulties, I made it home safely. To this day, I'm still a little afraid of snow, although I've learned to control that fear and to see past it.

As a child, what impressed me most about New York City were the parks. There were no parks in Port-au-Prince. Here, there were several in each neighbourhood. They were so safe that my mother allowed my sister and me to go alone. I just loved the atmosphere of the parks, of all the children playing freely. My sister and I would spend hours there.

The months I spent alone with my mother in Manhattan were the best times we ever shared. I was all she had; therefore, she was kind to me. We had a great life: we lived in a one-room apartment in a hotel adjacent to Central Park. Every Sunday we attended mass at St Patrick's Church, ate at a nearby Horn and Hardart cafeteria and attended the Radio City Music Hall matinee.

We had a second-hand TV and enjoyed watching the local programs. That's where I saw ballet for the first time and I loved it on sight. I'll never forget the first time, on another show, we saw white Americans dance. It was absolutely hilarious to see them move and my mother and I couldn't keep ourselves from laughing. They could hardly follow the beat.

Coming from a culture where people seem born with rhythm and can make the succession of movements of a dance flow seamlessly and harmoniously into one another, it was a complete surprise for us to see uncoordinated people whose movements were totally out of sync with the music.

Stability doesn't come easily for immigrants that are "fresh off the boat." When my father and sister joined us in New York, a friend advised my father to buy a pick-up truck with the savings he and my mother had managed to bring from Haiti. My mother was against the idea but my father was adamant.

The friend explained to my father that in New York it snows a lot. All he had to do was install a plow in front of the pick-up and get into the business of snow-clearing. It was guaranteed success and the money he would make would be enough to tide him over till the next winter.

Unfortunately, things didn't quite unfold that way, and a few months later my parents had to sell the pick-up to survive.

My mother could have worked as a dentist in New York. The State recognized her degree; the only requirement was that she passes the State exam to get a license.

A few men, who had been her classmates in Port-au-Prince, took the exam. One of them, with whom she was closer, was kind enough to share all the details regarding the application and persuaded her to register for the exam.

Swept by his enthusiasm, she did that and bought a couple of the books he had recommended to prepare; however, she never even opened the books and didn't show up on the day of the exam.

When her friend asked her why she hadn't taken it, she said she hadn't been notified as to when it would take place. He told her that her name was on the list at the door of the exam room. That night she made a scene claiming that, if she had missed the opportunity of writing the exam it was because of me.

Every day, when my sister and I returned from school, I would collect the mail from our mailbox and bring it to the apartment. Seizing the opportunity, my mother claimed that, she hadn't received the notice because I could not be relied on to accomplish the simplest of tasks. My intrinsic negligence caused me to misplace the envelope containing the crucial notice. She concluded by arguing passionately that my unreliability had robbed the family of this great opportunity for a better life.

I was twelve.

My father gazed at the floor and remained silent during her diatribe. I knew it was because he didn't believe her story for a second. But, he knew better than to confront my mother. It would achieve nothing and make matters worse.

Having missed a good opportunity, both my parents went from job to job, over the next ten years, hoping to improve their situation. Every single year we moved to be closer to the workplace of one of them, depending on the current circumstance. Throughout grade school and high school my sister and I changed school every single year. Every year we were the new kids at school.

In Haiti my parents were financially stable and had a great social life. In New York they had no social network and experienced instability. They were unhappy and the atmosphere at home was always tense. I found it difficult to be poor and worse to be called "nigger." I was now a Black child living in a "white" country.

My conjunctivitis was chronic.

Ten years after moving to New York, my father became ill. He decided to move back to Haiti permanently. My mother joined him a few months later. I was married, so I stayed in New York. My father died young.

Chapter 4: Being Disowned

The song "In the Summertime" was playing in the background on the radio the day I met Antoine. Family and friends called him "Tony." He did a couple of quick, well-synchronized little dance steps (clearly, he liked this song) and, with the warmest smile asked me, *comment vas-tu?* and kissed me, as is the custom for Haitians.

He had been to France several times and acquired a bit of a Parisian accent which he flaunted unapologetically. He smoked, his gestures imitating those of movie celebrities. He had a debonair look, but what captivated me most about Tony was his light lisp. Whenever he said a word that included the "s" sound, it sounded as though he kissed the word. Could anything be sexier? I was a goner.

I was sixteen.

Our families were of the same social background and had immigrated to the United States for the same reasons. We were both Haitian adolescents trying to find our footing in the American reality. Our staple was Haitian food. Haitian music made our hearts beat but we appreciated trendy rock as well. We both spoke perfect French. We were a match made in heaven.

Two years later Tony and I got married. "Controversial" doesn't begin to describe the circumstances surrounding our relationship, so we ended up eloping.

When I informed my parents that I had married Tony, they disowned me. My father called to speak to me. He said he and my mother wanted nothing to do with me for the remainder of their lives. That, if by chance, one day they and I should meet on the street, I'd better cross to the other side; they shouldn't have to suffer walking past me. Moreover, from that point onward, my mother would no longer be my mother nor he my father. He said a curt "goodbye," and hung up. Those were his last words to me. My father died without speaking to me again.

My family left New York shortly after that and returned to Haiti because, as my father had made clear in his call, my mother couldn't bear living in the same city I did.

The official story regarding my marriage was that my parents disapproved of Tony. However, I knew that the chaos they conjured around my wish to date him, and which led us to elope, had very little to do with that. They seized on our marriage because Tony and I happened to be in the right place at the right time to serve as their excuse and scapegoat for dealing with their problems.

As I mentioned earlier, my father returned to Haiti about ten years after we moved to the United States. He was tired of struggling economically and went back alone. A few months later he became ill and returned to New York for medical evaluation. He was diagnosed with cirrhosis of the liver. He bit the bullet like a man and decided he wanted to return to Haiti permanently.

Once back in Haiti, my father called my mother every Sunday. However, within a couple of months he began skipping the odd Sunday and my mother became edgy. She roamed the apartment complaining about his selfishness to put her through this worry; he was sick and anything could happen. But the "I'm-worried-about-his-health" routine didn't fool me. I knew exactly what she was worried about because I had seen it happen in the past.

Ten years before, about four months after my mother and I had arrived in New York, a family friend came to visit. In my presence he told her that although he was friends with both of them, he felt compelled, under the circumstances, to tell her that shortly after she and I had left Haiti my father began an affair with another woman. In his opinion, if my mother didn't do something about it quickly, she would lose her husband. She thanked him for warning her and he said his wife had convinced him it was the right thing to do.

I was only eight years old but I was all she had, so I was the one she talked to. After cursing my father, she got down to the task of how to remove him from the clutches of the other woman. She had a sharp mind and quickly came up with a solution.

There was a retired doctor who lived in our building. A couple of times when I was sick, he had agreed to see me and take care of me. She took my hand and went to knock at his door. He greeted us kindly, clearly expecting that I wasn't well. When my mother explained that our call had to do with another matter, he invited us in.

She outlined the details of her situation plainly and asked for his help. With the simplicity of a man who has experienced hardship, he assented. He immediately wrote to the United States Customs and Immigration Service stating that my mother was ill and alone with a child in New York City. It was imperative that her husband be allowed to join her as soon as possible. My mother thanked him; she looked revived.

She sent the letter to my father and told him to take it to the American Embassy to add to his application for an alien card. It worked. And that's how, five months later, he was granted authorization to enter the United States to join my mother and me.

I was no moron. Clearly, history was repeating itself; my father stopped calling regularly because he had a mistress and, as the cheating partner often unconsciously feels compelled to do in these circumstances, by not calling regularly, he was sending smoke signals to my mother to let her know something was up.

While this drama was going on, Tony and I had openly expressed our love for each other. In my innocence, I thought sharing this with my mother was the right thing to do. Bad choice!

Her reaction to the news that Tony and I loved each other played on several levels. First, she was thinking:

What, I'm losing my husband and you, you little shit, are telling me that you're in love? Really? Over my dead body will you get half a chance at happiness while I'm watching mine unravel!

I was pretty good at reading my mother. As they say, eyes tell and hers told me a lot.

Next, there was the layer that touched her image. My mother's opinion of Tony was tainted by her condescension toward his father, a journalist who had been publicly accused of plagiarism in Haiti. Despite his explanations that the newspaper had failed to include the necessary quotation marks, the charge stuck. "Like father, like son" she thought. Having her daughter associated with them would cause her to lose face publicly. What would people say? Again, over her dead body!

My mother was an intelligent woman and also very cunning. Cunning became the dominant element in her reaction. In a split second she saw how she could capitalize on my news to secure her husband. I watched and saw clearly as, in her mind, she went to the old tin cookie box where she stored her prized notes and pulled out the one for "Chaos." The neatly hand-written pages contained her fighting strategies. The notes were a family heritage, handed down through generations. They had proved their efficacy.

To begin my mother had a fit and forbade Tony and me to continue seeing each other. In the days that followed, if she could have torn me to shreds with her bare hands she would have. I was demeaned all day long.

It was summer vacation. I was off from school and worked full time as cashier at a corner store. While I was at work, I called Tony and told him what my mother was putting me through. That same weekend he came to reassure my mother that his intentions were serious; he wanted to marry me. My mother almost had a stroke and, beyond furious, told Tony to go home. However, her fury was just theatrics because Tony expressing his intentions conveniently brought grist to her mill.

After Tony left, my mother ranted bitterly. It was ugly. But I was used to ugly. From the day my sister was born my mother had no need for me in her life. Her pregnancy with my sister was very difficult. Afterwards, she was in a coma for a week. From the moment she held my sister in her arms I no longer existed. Even my father took second place in her life. In my sister she had found her soul mate.

From that point on, I was my mother's punching bag. Every frustration was taken out on me, delivered with rage and a look of disgust. She ended every diatribe with:

Look at you, look at your face, your mouth looks like an asshole.
Get out of my sight.

I grew up on ugly.

But, on the day Tony told my mother about his intentions, ugly hadn't been enough. When it came to me, the pain she inflicted always had to be extreme. She mobilized her anger and dark emotions in response to his declaration and dropped to her knees, raising her arms to the sky. Then, she lifted her head to implore the heavens in a voice vibrating with fervor:

> *God, here I am, kneeling before you, asking you to show me your mercy. God, grant me that, if Chérie marries Tony and has children, those children will die and she will be left holding their cold dead bodies in her arms.*

I was shaken to the core.

Satisfied that she had put the fear of God into me, and that I would do as I was told, she got down to the business of securing her husband. I was the key pawn in the scheme. Like an astute chess player who can coldly plan a strategy in detail, she decided to send me to another city to stay with an aunt, one she could browbeat and manipulate easily. The following day I was put on a *Greyhound* bus.

My mother despised all her relatives and this aunt was at the top of her hate list. A confirmed opportunist, like many Haitians, my mother subscribed to the philosophy *sot ki bay; enbesil ki pa pran* which means it's an idiot who gives; an imbecile who doesn't profit. She manipulated my aunt into taking me in and my aunt caved. My mother justified using people with no qualms.

After shipping me to my aunt, my mother called my father to tell him what his daughter was up to. She pushed his back to the wall and demanded that he come to New York to straighten things out. Suddenly, sparing my father stress on account of his poor health was no longer a concern. I realized that she would have made him swim from Haiti to New York to ensure that, in the end, he was present to do her bidding.

My mother's plan was simple: knock two birds with one stone. The stone was my father and, with him, she planned to eliminate the "other" woman and me, enemies who threatened to make her lose face publicly.

Chapter 5: The Deceit

A few days after my mother had sent me to my aunt's place my father came to New York. The official purpose of his trip was to separate me and Tony. His visit lasted three days. He spent two days with my mother, came to see me at my aunt's and flew back to Haiti the following day.

My father was a man of few words. Our conversation lasted five minutes or less. He expressed how deeply disappointed he was with me. His words shamed me profoundly. I had a boundless adoration for my father, and would have done anything to gain his approval. He told me to cut all ties with Tony.

My mother's curse about holding my dead children in my arms was still ringing in my ears. So, without complaining and in spite of the pain my decision caused me, I pushed my personal desires aside and chose to please my father. After I promised him that I would stop seeing Tony, he asked me to put it in writing in a letter addressed to Tony. I did as I was told.

Totally dispirited, I asked my aunt for an envelope, inserted the letter and sealed it. When I handed it to my father, I asked him for a favor. I admitted that when I arrived at my aunt's I had called Tony to let him know where I was so that he wouldn't worry.

I therefore asked my father to mail the letter from Haiti, explaining that when Tony received my letter, he would try to get in touch with me, even come to my aunt's place to understand what had happened.

If the envelope is mailed from Haiti, Tony will think I had moved there with you, I told my father.

I figured it would make it easier for Tony to move on if he thought I now lived in Haiti. My father agreed and put the letter in his shirt pocket.

The following morning, when my aunt and I accompanied my father to the taxi that would take him to the airport, I saw them exchange a knowing look accompanied by a light nod. I wondered about it but couldn't figure out what it meant. We said our goodbyes and my father kissed me on the top of the head, as he liked to do. My aunt and I stood on the sidewalk for a moment to watch the taxi drive away.

Three days later, while my aunt was at work, Tony called. He told me he had received my letter and was calling to find out what was going on. I was mortified. While I was trying to work out how he received the letter so quickly, I heard him ask,

Since when do you misspell your name?
What? What? What are you talking about? I asked.

The person who signed my name at the bottom of the letter he was holding had written Chérie, without "e" at the end.

Tony read the letter to me. It wasn't my letter. In an instant, everything clicked. I now understood the "look" I had intercepted between my aunt and my father. He had turned my letter over to her and she had been put in charge of taking care of business. The "look" and the nod were to confirm to my father that she had things in hand.

Clearly, my mother was behind all this. My aunt would never have opened my letter, re-written it and signed it without my mother's strict instructions. My aunt, who had been in the USA for over twenty-five years, had practically lost her French, so she didn't realize she'd misspelled my name. Ironically, she was my godmother and was the one who had chosen it.

I had been duped by my father. "Not my father, not my father" my heart cried. I was crushed. I had believed until then that my father loved me. I had also believed his word meant something. I guess, on that occasion, self-interest prevailed over integrity.

Right then and there I lost all respect for my father.

As for my mother, that she would scheme behind my back was a given. The irony of the situation was that, during all the years that she had raised me, she had always stipulated that "a person's correspondence was sacred." In this instance, it was apparently a case of "do-as-I-say, not-as-I-do." Her hypocrisy made me sick to my stomach.

In light of my parents' duplicity, I asked Tony to help me leave my aunt's place. His response was:

Let's get married my love.

Yes, I said.

Could a marriage proposal be any more romantic?

Within an hour Tony called me back; he had found a place for me to go to. Taking only my purse, I went to the address he gave me. When my aunt came back home from work, I was gone.

We knew my aunt would be worried, so that same evening, shortly after she got home from work, Tony's brother called to let her know I was safe. He asked my aunt for my ID card so that I could return home. She had confiscated it the minute I had arrived at her place. My aunt told him to discuss the matter with my mother. He called my mother and she said she didn't have my card. They stonewalled him.

Contrary to what she would later claim, my mother didn't spend days worrying about my safety. There is no doubt my aunt called her as soon as she arrived home to let her know I was gone. I am also certain that as soon as she finished talking with Tony's brother, she called my mother back to let her know I was safe. Therefore, within an hour of my aunt discovering I was gone, she and my mother both knew I was neither lost nor in danger.

In spite of that, the following day my aunt filed a Missing Person report with the Police. She gave them the address of every relative I had in the city so that they could verify whether I was with them. After being visited by police officers, all my relatives were beside themselves with worry thinking I was lost in a city I didn't know.

They later learned through my aunt that I fled because I wanted to be with Tony. Except for one aunt, my relatives strongly disapproved of my behavior, and blamed me for being insubordinate, inconsiderate and selfish. Something broke between them and me and our relationship was never the same after that. Our connection became superficial, even with the aunt and uncle who had adored me when I was little. The general consensus behind my back was: "like mother, like daughter".

My mother knew I was safe, yet she forced my aunt to file a Missing Person report with the Police. It was by design. This was calculated to satisfy her thirst for drama, to spark family-wide concern and, most importantly, to cast herself in the role of victim, shielding her from potential attacks or losing face. She was a "Mother in Distress."

The irony was that, because my mother's family had disapproved of my father, she and he had eloped. She had always hated all her relatives but, with that rejection, her hatred reached new heights and festered. Over the years, she only connected with them when absolutely necessary or when she needed a pawn she could manipulate for her purposes.

My mother playing the role of victim over my alleged disappearance effectively muzzled my relatives. Had anyone been inclined to express concern or, God forbid, point out the irony of her behavior given the circumstances of her own marriage, she would have attacked them for kicking a frantically worried mother when she was already down.

There is no doubt in my mind that my mother was certain I had sought refuge with one of my relatives and she was itching to know which one, but calling them to inquire about my whereabouts would have been beneath her.

While she didn't care about my aunt's opinion, the one she had sent me to, this wasn't the case for some of her other relatives, particularly the older ones. She may have hated them, but she knew she could not manipulate them or pull the wool over their eyes. Approaching them directly regarding my whereabouts would be admitting she had lost control over her daughter. Using the Police reshuffled things in her favour.

With her negative but incisive mind, my mother saw using the Police as an excellent opportunity to throw her relatives into temporary turmoil; she wasn't going to waste a chance to rattle, trouble, and/or devastate.

She knew her relatives would genuinely worry about me. Mostly, she knew that, if they had sheltered me and were exposed by the Police, they would be humiliated and terrified at the prospect of my mother's ensuing wrath and the potential legal consequences.

Sending the Police after my relatives was, for my mother, a treasure trove of everything negative. She knew that just an officer's presence at their door would deeply upset them, even if momentarily. When you have lived through a bloody dictatorship, Police evoke only bad news, as she knew from firsthand experience. It was therefore a scare tactic. Through the Police my mother was flexing her muscles at her relatives.

I suspect she was already scripting her rebuke to the relative for when the Police would discover who had sheltered me.

If using the Police didn't wreak the havoc she had intended, she could always plead that, driven by worry over my disappearance, she had done what any mother would do under the circumstances.

Anticipating my mother's actions, I had specifically asked Tony to find me a place with no link to family.

One week after I left my aunt's place Tony and I were married. The following day, I informed my parents. Clearly, my mother had again forced my father to return to New York because he was the one who made that fateful phone call to cut me off from their lives. It was not a long-distance from Haiti; it was a local call.

My mother had won. In her view, I had received the best possible retribution: I was out of her life for good and, in addition, as far as she knew, no longer had relatives I could count on.

The only person who stood by Tony and me for our marriage was his older brother. I will forever be grateful for his support.

And "the other woman?" Like me, she was eliminated. My mother reclaimed her husband and went back to Haiti to live with my father.

Years later I learned about the lies my parents concocted about the hardship I had allegedly put them through with my marriage to Tony: Not having found me after visiting my relatives, the Police would have turned over my file to the FBI. Immediately, the FBI would have summoned my father and put him through a grueling interrogation; during that very same week, my father would have received an anonymous phone call demanding ransom money for my release, money which he would have delivered as asked.

We are to understand that, during the handful of days my father spent in New York after being summoned from Haiti by my mother because I had supposedly disappeared, since the Police had not found me with any of my relatives, they would have turned my file over to the FBI.

And, the FBI began investigating my case by questioning my father – only my father. They didn't get in touch with my aunt, my mother, Tony or his brother. Anyone who had seen a few Police Procedurals on TV would have assumed that at least Tony might have been a person of interest, if not the main suspect, in the matter .... Clearly, the version put forth by my parents defied all logic ...

The "pièce de resistance" to the story was the purported demand for ransom in exchange for my release.

My "disappearance" gave my mother the upper hand. I can see her demonstrating to my father how I had disobeyed them both and repeating "your-daughter-disrespected-you."

Do anything to a Haitian man, but don't "disrespect" him. A Haitian man who believes he has been disrespected will go to any lengths to reclaim his honor. He will cut-off his own right arm if he believes it will restore his dignity. Having struck that sensitive nerve, my mother would have had him exactly where she wanted him: cornered, in a chokehold, having no choice but to do any and all her bidding.

So, when he returned to New York after my alleged disappearance, my father knew he had lost the battle and that my mother would be going back to Haiti with him. Forsaking me had sealed the deal.

He therefore had no interest in extending his stay, especially with the issue of the "other woman" to deal with before my mother's arrival in Haiti. He stayed in the City for only a few days.

Which means that the alleged Police/FBI/kidnapping events could only have occurred inside a five-day window, at most. If that were the case, my father would have received the ransom call within hours before or after he was "called-in by the FBI for questioning."

If he received the hypothetical "call" before or after the interview, did he tell the FBI? I will venture that the answer to the question is No. Had he mentioned "kidnapping" to the FBI, I doubt they'd have chalked it up to "family matter" and closed the file, as the story states.

If memory serves, the amount allegedly requested by the imaginary kidnapper was three thousand US dollars in cash.

Did I, Tony or his brother engineer a plan to extort money from my father? No. Who knew about our circumstances? Only family. For the sake of argument, let's consider the possibility that one of my mother's relatives decided to take advantage of the situation to play a dirty trick on my parents.

If that was the case, why would my father play along? Why would he, as the story claims, put three thousand dollars in a suitcase and deliver it to the street specified by a kidnapper when he knew for a fact that I wasn't "missing;" I was with Tony.

Moreover, in those days, three thousand dollars was a lot of money. My parents had no savings to speak of. So, where, at the drop of a hat, would my father find that money?

If he did have that money, had he travelled with the cash in his back pocket when he flew to New York, miraculously ready before the kidnapper even asked for it?

Another incongruity in the tale was my father's supposed reaction: would a practical man like him have been so readily and rapidly manipulated by the "kidnapper"? He was far from gullible or stupid.

I sometimes wonder whether my parents considered this chapter in later years, and had any misgivings, regrets or even embarrassment about their actions.

Chapter 6: My Marriage

My marriage to Tony was romance-novel-material.

I began our married life empty-handed, with only the clothes I had on my back.

Because Tony's older brother knew the priest personally, we were granted a dispensation from the customary publication of banns, and were married within a few days. The priest was young, and his heart was touched by our story. He knew first-hand how conservative Haitian parents could be, and wanted to do his part in supporting true love.

Three people attended our wedding ceremony: the two witnesses and Tony's brother. The priest was kind; he realized how shy I was and didn't insist that I speak. He took care of all the talking and his words were uplifting. Our two friends who acted as witnesses congratulated Tony and me warmly for believing in and standing by each other.

I wore a little dress I had bought in the basement of a bargain outlet for $6.99. The dominant colour was light green with pink motifs. I had heard that green and pink was a lucky color combination, so in my eyes, it was the perfect and most beautiful dress. For my makeup I wore just a tiny bit of almost-colourless lipstick. Tony was wearing his only pair of dress pants and a blue jacket that suited him very well.

I thought we made a wonderful couple and was the happiest bride in the whole wide world.

After the ceremony the six of us went to Tony's brother's apartment where a couple of Tony's other friends joined us. His brother's girlfriend had prepared a nice table with cheese, crackers, some cut vegetables, a couple bottles of wine and some soft drinks. It was the first time I'd met her and was deeply touched. In addition to being generous and caring, she was absolutely delightful.

We spent the afternoon laughing and joking about this and that, stories mostly related to life in Haiti. The mood was lively. In those days I was extremely shy, so I didn't contribute much to the conversation, but I enjoyed listening to the cheerful banter. Tony kept his arm around me the whole time.

Later that evening, we went to a live music bar downtown with Tony's brother and his girlfriend. It was my first time in a bar. We enjoyed the music and danced. Tony and I danced perfectly in sync, as if we had done it all our lives.

Can a wedding celebration get any better?

Tony was charm personified and handsome to boot. I had difficulty expressing myself because of my extreme shyness, but Tony spoke with ease and elegance. He was well-read and could discuss most topics effortlessly, including world politics; he was particularly passionate about Haitian politics.

He believed in social justice and felt compelled to participate in public demonstrations about human rights issues. My admiration knew no bounds. He had traveled considerably and was worldly. He had so many interesting stories about France and Africa. He excelled at social graces.

Why this wonderful young man gave someone as ordinary as me a second look I will never know. I had such a low opinion of myself that I was convinced no boy would ever be interested in me. At sixteen I had accepted I wasn't worthy of being loved, and would spend the rest of my life alone.

When Tony had started showing signs of interest in me I was truly taken aback. Slowly we became friends and, despite my overwhelming self-consciousness, he won me over bit by bit, so the day he told me he loved me, I believed him.

Someone loved me wholeheartedly. He made me feel special, cherished. I was the most important person to someone. I was filled with hope and security. I could hardly believe my luck.

When we were alone Tony flirted with me in the most romantic ways. One day, he bought a single coin-shaped chocolate wrapped in gold foil and told me that if he had any gold, he would lay it at my feet.

He only had this gold-foil covered chocolate coin to offer but he hoped I could see it was more valuable than real gold because it carried all his love for me. When he went on like this, I would melt like a pat of butter under a hot midday sun.

In the end, I put so much confidence in Tony's love that I found the determination to push aside my self-consciousness and deep insecurities. I opened my heart and my arms wide for him, without reservation. What I wanted most was to be his. I loved him so much I would have trusted him with my life. My intentions were pure and when I said "I love you" I meant it.

Tony was so affectionate. He would tell me "I love you" a million times every day. I believed him every time. Against all odds, life had given me a second chance.

I remember thanking whatever star had bestowed this good luck upon me. I was confident that everything would be fine from this point onward because I would never be alone again. I had someone who loved me and we would face life together.

Our day-to-day life was wonderful. Tony had a full-time job. I had contacted my former employer and he had taken me back as cashier at his corner store. During the remainder of the summer, until university resumed in September, I worked there full time.

We had our little routine. On Saturday mornings Tony would drink his first cup of coffee and then we would go to a nearby bakery to get fresh, warm cinnamon rolls. They were the best in the world. They weren't the common chunky, doughy rolls. These were thin because the dough was no thicker than a finger. The roll was soft and light on the inside while the caramelized cinnamon sugar coating was crispy. By the time we got home, Tony and I would have eaten half of them.

I would cook a Haitian breakfast of onion-filled omelet and grilled buttered bread. Tony would have a second cup of coffee. I didn't like coffee but enjoyed dunking my grilled bread lightly in his coffee. We laughed as we dusted bread crumbs from each other's lips. The radio was always on. We knew all the "chansonettes françaises" by heart and sang along joyfully.

Because we worked, we could afford to go to the movie theater, which we loved. I remember we saw *Harold and Maude* that summer. When it didn't rain, we would go for long walks in the evenings. Hand in hand, we would envision the life we wanted to build together. It included children.

On Friday nights we had pizza. Don't ask me how we did it, but we managed to devour an extra-large pizza. In our defense, it was excellent pizza! Another one of our favorite treats was *Dairy Queen* ice cream.

I decorated the apartment. We got a few pieces of second-hand furniture which I stripped and repainted. With some cheap but well-chosen prints for the walls and little things like cushion covers and lamp shades that I made by hand, our place looked like a warm home.

About a month after we were married, the aunt I was close to made the effort to come and visit. She was worried about us. We had spoken on the phone after my wedding, but she had wanted to see us with her own eyes to make sure we were fine. She only stayed a weekend, but her visit made a world of difference in our lives.

Tony's brother had been there for us, but he was our age. Having an aunt openly show her support by visiting us and saying that we could always count on her for anything meant the world to us.

During her visit my aunt took the time to teach me two essential Haitian dishes: *pâté* and *tarte à l'oignon*. The latter would become my signature dish. The love she displayed towards me while we cooked together made my heart overflow.

She told me stories about how her own mother had always been too impatient to teach her how to cook anything. She had learned from the mothers of her friends. Although she's gone, I still have the little sheet of paper where she had written the recipe for *pâté* and she will always be one of the people I loved most in this life. I will carry her in my heart until the day I die.

Her visit had a deep impact on Tony and me. Being forsaken by my parents had been a hard blow. Somehow, the support of my aunt legitimized our love. We felt accepted. We were no longer totally ostracized. We felt stronger.

What I loved most about my relationship with Tony was our intimacy. Tony loved reading. He had several books sitting on the night table, waiting to be read. When he read, I would lie with my head in his lap and he would read out loud for my benefit. We would spend hours like this. Often, we would stop to discuss a passage in the book and exchange views on what we thought about the author's ideas. Between paragraphs Tony would kiss me.

At night, when we went to bed, I sang for Tony while caressing him softly. I knew a lot of French lullabies and would sing all of them for him. One evening I initiated the routine of telling a story. It was about a boy and a girl who were never supposed to fall in love, but did. They had to fight for their love and, despite the challenges they faced, love won and they lived happily ever after. It didn't take long for Tony to participate in the story-telling and invent his versions of the same fairy tale. These moments were pure magic.

I will always remember the first night we spent together. We lay in Tony's small single bed, bodies tightly wrapped together, and promised each other we would never let go.

Chapter 7: Six Weeks

We were still newlyweds when, just for fun, Tony and I planned that I would meet him at his workplace at the end of the day so we could enjoy the pleasure of going back home together. It was a Friday and I arrived at the office where he worked just before closing. I identified myself to the receptionist and she let Tony know I was there.

He came to the lobby without delay and welcomed me warmly and affectionately. He looked genuinely happy to see me. God, I loved him. Every time I saw him, I counted my blessings. I was the luckiest girl in the whole world. I loved him so much I became giddy just at the sight of him. He held my hands and I felt overjoyed at the simple prospect of spending the weekend in his company.

Just as Tony was about to go back inside to wrap things up for the day a young woman entered the lobby from the same door Tony had used. He invited her to join us, to introduce me. She acted delighted. Our conversation was short but pleasant. She said goodbye, wished us a good weekend and, with a confident stride, headed back inside.

When she went directly back inside it struck me that the only reason she had come to the lobby was to see me. I figured Tony had mentioned my arrival. I was touched by the idea, and a nice warmth filled my heart. As for the young woman, I surmised that curiosity had gotten the better of her and she couldn't resist coming to the lobby to take a peek at her co-worker's new bride.

But my thoughts changed drastically when I caught Tony turning aside in order to have a better view of the young woman as she was sashaying away. In a split second I went from feeling warm and fuzzy to shell-shocked. Tony was looking at the young woman with undiluted desire. I watched dumbstruck as his blatant lascivious glance slowly caressed her receding body from head to heel and back up. His eyes remained glued to her until she disappeared behind the door.

I died on the spot.

All kinds of alarm bells went off inside me and excruciatingly painful traps snapped shut on parts of my inside. Instinctively I realized that the young woman had only come to check me out and, if the confidence with which she sauntered off was any indication, I had been assessed and found wanting.

Despite the harrowing pain slicing through me, I was clear-minded enough to recognize that she wasn't wrong in her assessment. I was no match for this self-assured, sophisticated, sexy woman. She was wearing high heels and a beautiful dress. Her fingers were prettily manicured, her haircut was sharp, and her makeup was flawless. Here I was, an 18-year-old girl wearing cheap flip-flops and jeans with a plain blouse, my finger and toe nails were trim and bare, my hair was arranged in a homely braid and my face was naked. I didn't have a chance in hell.

The tiny bit of feminine self-confidence I had was instantly obliterated.

Finally, when the door closed and the young woman was out of view, Tony casually turned back toward me, looked me in the eye and held my stare. He realized I had been watching him closely the whole time, absorbing the scene. I am certain that the devastation and anguish I was experiencing were written all over my face. He, however, looked coolly composed. I saw his indifference to seeing that I understood what had just happened, and knew that he had intended for me to see it all.

I went into a tailspin.

I saw, in my mind's eye and felt in my bones, the free fall and the ensuing crash. I was completely destroyed. But somehow, concurrently, as if two realities had overlapped, and coming from I-don't-know-where, I felt a Force inside me. It was powerful; its dominant energy was compassion. The force caught me, held me firmly and, against all logic, prevented the aforementioned freefall and crash. I breathed jerkily.

While I remained enfolded in the protective energy of the Compassionate Force, another force, stepped in. Its energy was totally different: shrewd, combative and ruthless. This force was all about survival. Almost against my will, it kept my senses and my wits on alert. Sharp insight flooded my mind. I felt as if I'd been given a hawk's vision.

Looking at Tony with this hawk-like sight, I saw him adjust his gaze from aloof to a mix of aplomb and defiance. As if nothing had happened, he invited me to sit, indicating he'd be back shortly. Right before my eyes, he grew a few inches taller, exuded pseudo-Alpha-male vibes and radiated self-appreciation. I was flabbergasted.

The change in his body language wouldn't have been more obvious if he had pulled a super-hero cape out of thin air and swirled it dramatically over his shoulders. Totally in character, cape a-floating, he swaggered across the lobby and disappeared behind the same door as the young woman. If it hadn't been tragic, it would have been funny. I failed to see the humour.

With heightened awareness I considered what had just happened and reality hit me like a tsunami. If, to my face, Tony felt perfectly entitled to ogle another woman the way he had looked at this one, with no qualms about doing it openly, he didn't love me.

On the heels of that realization came another devastating certainty. Tony had actually enjoyed doing what he'd done; he got a high from humiliating me. A merciless undertow dragged me down under and raked every inch of my body over razor sharp rocks.

I understood right then and there that my marriage was a big mistake. I didn't want to survive this shock.

Lifeless doesn't begin to describe how I felt. During the few minutes I sat waiting for Tony in the lobby my whole world came crashing down around my ears: marital bliss had lasted six weeks.

I was no stranger to agonising shock, but this one hit me hard. On the inside, I was dying a very painful death. The Compassionate Force helped me breathe and compose myself.

For the life of me, I hadn't seen that one coming.

On the bus ride home, I was incapable of speech and must have been pale as a ghost. In stark contrast Tony looked totally relaxed. For the whole ride he ignored me and read his newspaper. His callous indifference hit me in a place where it hurt excruciatingly.

As they say: "it's not the stab in the back that kills you; it's seeing who's holding the knife when you turn around."

That evening, although all I wanted was to shut my eyes tight and die, the Shrewd Force compelled me to keep my eyes open and pay close attention to Tony. As I observed him, I realized he was aware of being watched and enjoyed it. The Shrewd Force had claws. It held my head in a viselike grip to keep me from looking away and said,

What do you see?

I wanted to turn and run but the force was a thousand times stronger. I had no choice but to look and to see. I saw, I understood, I acknowledged.

Putting the pieces together, the picture was strikingly clear: Tony knew exactly what he had done. He had set the ground rules for our marriage and was damn proud of himself.

What else? The force asked.

"I realize he doesn't love me," I admitted, doubling over in pain on the inside.

The Shrewd Force released me, understanding I needed to howl the feral wail I could no longer contain. On the inside, I shrieked like a wounded animal. I screamed until I was totally spent. A feeling of hollowness settled in me. I didn't need further evidence to admit the truth: I was in love with someone who didn't love me.

I will never recover from this.

We had made plans to have pizza that evening. Around a mouthful of pizza Tony looked at me with feigned innocence and said,

you're very quiet, what's wrong?

In a millisecond I assessed my situation. I realized I was totally spent. I couldn't find a drop of energy to defend myself, even if my life depended on it. So, I took the coward's way out, sidestepped the issue, and said I had a motion sickness headache from the bus ride.

As I said it, I could see in Tony's eyes he knew very well that I was evading the question. With a hint of a smirk on his lips, he nodded as if to say: "good answer, blame whatever it is you're feeling on motion sickness."

As he dug into the pizza hungrily, I read the subtext: "I'm a man; I do what I want with whom I want."

In the days that followed I contemplated the truth of my reality. While the broken hearted 16-year-old-me who had fallen head over heels in love with Tony was shrieking in agony, I, 18-year-old-me, sat up to take stock of our situation. A trap door had opened under the feet of both of us and we had fallen to the bottom of the pit of despair.

It wasn't the first time I had landed in the pit. But this time, it seemed deeper, too deep to escape, and the despair seemed too dark, beyond the reach of any light. All the hopes and dreams of my 16-year-old-self and me had been crushed. The short film of how Tony had, in our presence, taken all the time he wanted to look at another woman, displaying his appreciation openly, played over and over on the common screen of our minds, the meaning of the images cutting more viciously each time. The screams of pain and fear from my 16-year-old-self were paralyzing.

Tony had never looked at us as he had the young woman, and he never would.

16-year-old and I had no-one to turn to. I considered approaching my parents to ask them to take us back. I knew they would accept. I also knew that once 16-year-old and I returned my parents would laugh at us so hard they would bring the house down. They would not see in me a little girl seeking support and solace. Compassion was not their forte.

And, when they'd laughed their fill, I would be ridiculed and demeaned every day, at every opportunity. The whole family would have a field day bullying me.

There would have been no limits to the humiliation and cruelty I, and by extension 16-year-old, would have to endure. Eventually, having been dehumanized, we'd succumb to the unbearable suffering. We would die with our tail between our legs.

Other than our parents, 16-year-old and I had no one. The aunt who loved me, the one who had visited shortly after my marriage, was a young widow fighting to raise her children alone. We could not impose on her. There was no place to turn for shelter. 16-year-old and I had to face the music.

The fear this realization created was unfathomable. "God, please give us strength," I prayed. I stared into nothing for a moment, buying a few seconds of respite. But, dancing around the issue wasn't going to make the problem go away.

Finally, with the hopelessness of one condemned to death, I accepted that it was time to openly admit the finality of our situation. I expelled a long sigh. The Shrewd Force helped me square my shoulders. With unwavering lucidity, 18-year-old-me stated the obvious out loud for the benefit of 16-year-old.

> *The fault sits squarely with us.*
> *We chose Tony.*
> *We made our bed.*

As I uttered the words, I realized I was standing alone. 16-year-old was nowhere in sight. She had abandoned me. I hadn't seen that one coming either.

Standing alone, I realized how naïve I had been to believe in second chances. Self-deprecation doesn't begin to describe the shame I felt. Pondering what lay ahead, "I will surely die of broken heartedness," I thought. "But at least this way I will die with my head up." Suddenly, 18-year-old me felt old and spent. "What's done is done," she thought. "We cannot turn back; our only option is to bite the bullet."

My love story with Tony had ended. "Make the best of a bad situation" became my life mantra.

From that point on, our marriage was no longer a magical love story. The bedtime lullaby-singing and fairy-tale-telling ceased. To my deep sorrow, our relationship became the ordinary arrangement of most marriages: tacit complicity based on a common culture, joint interests, shared tastes in books and music, a sense of duty and some affection. As husband and wife, we were bound by a common life. We both preferred to avoid confrontation, which made the arrangement bearable.

I had believed that what Tony and I had was special. I was wrong.

Chapter 8: Post-partum Depressions

Is there anything worse for a woman than to feel abandoned while holding her newborn child? I went through it twice.

My first pregnancy was five years into my marriage and it was marked by Heather. I met her one day when I stopped by the office where Tony worked at the end of the day. He had found a better job and had been working there since about six months. He led around the office and introduced me to his boss and co-workers.

We got to Heather last and stayed with her longer than with the others. Tony stepped toward her, extended his hand and lightly touched her on the arm. His hand remained there one second longer than necessary making the touch almost a caress. He moved slightly to stand closer to her than to me. She hadn't flinched or acted the least surprised by his touch. Clearly, she was used to being touched by him.

As innocuous and as simple the touch may have appeared on the surface, I could see that it was loaded with meaning and intent. It was an unspoken message to Heather saying: "she's my wife, yes, and I can't change that, but it's you I'm choosing to touch right now, because it's you I love."

As for me, the purpose of the touch was to confirm: "yes, what you see is exactly right. I'm with Heather."

I was three months pregnant.

When we got home, I shared my observations of what I had seen with Tony. He stared at me wide-eyed, as if shocked. He raised his arms and then dropped them to his sides as if in total defeat and loudly exclaimed, *really?* while pacing a tight circuit to manifest his indignation, window-dressing the pacing with every exasperated gesture in his repertoire, all dramatically punctuated by well-timed pauses for sharp drags from his cigarette.

The man had a flair for theatrics and he made the most of every opportunity I provided to display his showmanship.

He repeated his original "Really?" with even more emphasis.

I don't believe it! He continued.

I extended my hand in a gesture of politeness and you blow it out of proportion and spin a convoluted tale out of it. What a bunch of baloney! You're such an insecure woman.

He went on and on and on until his imagination ran out of ideas on different ways of proving how insecure I am. I remained silent.

Because you're pregnant, I'll let it slide and chalk it up to hormones talking, he concluded.

In the end, I was left thoroughly humiliated. In the days that followed, I had to suffer his mocking glances. Throughout the whole pregnancy, every time he came home from work smiling uncontrollably, I knew Heather had put that smile on his lips. After a few minutes, his joy would dissipate and he would retreat behind his newspaper.

Heather was pretty, shy and had strikingly beautiful blond hair that fell past her waist. What Tony and Heather had was based on stolen moments because he came directly home from work every day and never slept out. There were certainly the occasional times when he was able to pretend he was going to Karate practice, for example, but instead spent a few hours with her, and they probably found short moments during their lunch hour.

The loneliness I felt after I realized Tony was with Heather was devastating. It permeated my soul and remained with me for the rest of the pregnancy.

Six months later, coming from the hospital with my first baby proved to be one of the most difficult experiences of my life. Tony had technically taken the week off from work to be with me, however, he made sure he was out all day long, every single day during those seven days.

The feelings of abandonment I lived through were so deep that the experience tore my fragile soul to shreds.

Tony literally broke me that week.

I left the hospital and returned home on a Monday morning. Tony came to pick me up accompanied by his mother. Shortly after dropping the baby and me at home, he left with her. She needed to run a few errands and after that she wanted him to go pick up his two younger sisters from school. Really? But I was too proud to object. And, I was deeply hurt that Tony prioritized being attentive to his mother's needs over taking care of the baby and me.

That week, public buses were on strike. My mother-in-law decided that since Tony was "free," he should drive his sisters to and from school every day, morning and afternoon. Their schools were half a mile and one mile away from their home; there was no reason the girls couldn't walk to school, but Tony and his mother had an unspoken agreement, and every day they came up with reasons for Tony to leave me alone.

During that week, until Friday, Tony left the baby and me early in the morning. After dropping his sisters at school, he would take his mother to run errands; then they would have lunch together. He would stay with her until it was time to pick up his sisters after school. Then, because she had cooked and he didn't want to offend her, he would have supper at his mother's. By the time he returned home in the evening, he was tired and needed to read his newspaper.

Saturday morning Tony left before dawn to take his mother to the airport because she was going to Haiti for a few weeks. He didn't return home until late afternoon. By then, I was beyond exhausted.

I had a caesarean birth and holding my baby when breastfeeding was difficult. I developed severe pain in my lower back.

When Tony returned home Saturday afternoon, I told him about my back pain and how exhausted I was. I begged him not to go out on

Sunday, to stay with me the whole day. He agreed. However, about an hour later one of his younger brothers called to ask him for a drive early the following morning to a nearby city and back. Tony agreed. When I reminded him that he had promised to stay with me, he replied that his brother needed him. At that moment, my back literally and figuratively broke, and even today it hasn't mended.

During that same week, everything about Tony's behavior confirmed my suspicions, which had begun shortly after I became pregnant, that he was having an affair with Heather.

I was in physical and emotional anguish.

The following week Tony went back to work; when he arrived home at night, he claimed he had had a stressful day at work, was too tired to help and needed rest. On the Saturday, I was in debilitating pain with my back. I let him sleep until noon and then woke him; I needed help with the baby.

He was immediately furious, and started screaming that he had worked hard all week and couldn't even get a moment's peace to rest. Radiating resentment, he lit a cigarette, pulled out his newspaper, and avoided me and the baby for the rest of the day.

One day, a few weeks later, Tony came home from work with a conspicuous hickey on his neck. I asked him about it. With his usual aplomb, he said it was the baby who sucked his neck. Right! I guess, feeling jealous about the baby, Heather had felt the need to make her presence known.

What I went through a few years later for my second pregnancy was worst. Tony had a knack for outdoing himself.

I was seven months pregnant with my second baby when my father died. An uncle relayed the news of his passing. It seemed my mother was too busy to call me herself. Nevertheless, I decided to attend the funeral. I took the first flight to Haiti, but missed the funeral by a few hours.

My intention was to stay with my mother about five days, but when I called home on the third day, he was distant and curt. My woman's intuition was well honed by then; I knew something was up. I asked my family to take me to the airport the following day, fingers crossed that I would get a seat on the flight, since it wasn't my scheduled departure date. I made it.

Everything that could go wrong on that flight did, and the delays kept adding up. By the time I reached New York City it was very late at night and my ankles were the same size as my knees. I called Tony from the airport to ask if he had any cash to pay for my taxi. Gruffly, he said he had no money, to go spend the night at his mother's house; it was closer to the airport. I would have preferred to spend the night on a bench out in the open.

I took a chance with a taxi. The driver was Haitian and I asked in Creole if, for twenty dollars, he would take me home. He took in my condition and said he would do it with pleasure.

When I got home, I found Tony with a woman. I opened the door of the room they were in and found them casually sitting on the floor Indian-style. His arms were sexily wrapped around her neck and his lips were an inch away from hers. When he turned his gaze toward me, his eyes were cloudy with sexual desire; they were primed for love-making. Would you believe the man had the gall, while his arms were still wrapped around the woman's neck, to smile and say to me, as if nothing was going on:

Oh! hi there, come on in.

I told him I would be one too many and left them.

I closed myself in another room and would have screamed like an animal if I could; instead, I cried in silence.

Needless to say, Tony never, ever asked me how I felt about my father's passing. I was over fifty when I finally grieved his loss.

That night I decided to leave Tony. I couldn't bear any more pain. Although we spent the night in different rooms and didn't speak, he must have sensed he was in hot water because the following day he called the aunt I was close to, to inform her of what had happened. He knew she was the only relative I was intimate with and the one person that had real influence on me.

When my aunt called me, I immediately realized he must have begged her to help him fix things. Before I let her speak, I told her I was leaving Tony. She saw things differently and, figuratively, sat me down and asked hard questions.

What do you think you're going to achieve by taking to the street when you're just about to pop while your first baby barely reaches your knees? Where will you go, to a woman's shelter? And from there, what? Welfare? That's the future you're going to offer your children?

Listen to me, she said, *you have no one to turn to for support. Grow up! Every woman endures exactly what you're going through. They brace themselves and deal with it. You married a Haitian man; what did you expect? Stop whining and face your responsibilities*!

In my heart I'd hoped she'd have said "baby darling, come to me. I'm there for you." But I realized it was unfair of me to think that; her plate was already full with her own life.

I stayed with Tony, but I was an empty shell.

As the saying goes, "when it rains, it pours." Two months later I delivered my second baby by caesarean as well. But this time the anesthesia didn't work. I realized something was wrong when, although I couldn't open my eyes, I could distinctly hear the voices of the medical staff chatting and felt a tube going down my throat. I gagged slightly. And then, I felt the coldness of the liquid the doctor used to wipe down my abdomen.

I panicked, but I couldn't move. I couldn't do anything to alert the staff to the fact that I wasn't asleep. I tried to stop breathing, but I couldn't. I was fully awake when the doctor cut me open. It's futile to try to describe the agony.

After being wheeled back to my bed I told Tony the anesthesia hadn't kicked in on time. He sighed deeply, lifted both arms and dropped them to his sides in a gesture of hopelessness, and shook his head as if to say: "I don't know what to tell you." Then he left the room; he needed to smoke.

During the years that followed, my relationship with Tony was downright toxic. I became emotionally dependent, always hoping to fix things between us. He became compulsively unfaithful; however, he made sure I would never catch him red-handed again. Every time I expressed my suspicion of his infidelity he would laugh in my face. As the years went by, he laughed harder and harder. But I still stayed.

I had zero self-respect.

Chapter 9: Elle

One day, a few years later, I had errands to run and Tony had "things to do." On the street a few hours later, I came face to face with Tony and Elle. For a millisecond, they froze in surprise; I registered their shock and froze as well. We scrambled to adjust our expressions to control what we were feeling, and the three of us recovered quickly enough to save face. We managed to smile; I gave them "A+" on the radiance of their expressions.

Recognizing my internal panic, my heartbeat went into overdrive and my mind faltered. On the inside, I lost my footing on the edge of an imaginary precipice. My arms wind-milled in a desperate attempt to break my emotional fall, but I went down. I heard my screams echo in the distance. The part of my mind that had remained alert read the subtle signs of the tension stealing through the two of them. The fleeting hints of stress confirmed that, like me, they were floundering on the inside.

Despite our best efforts, I felt certain that, to a discerning eye, the three of us looked conspicuous as hell.

In situations like this, time stops; but only a second had passed. By silent mutual agreement, we went into "let's-act-as-if-everything-is-okay" mode. We shuffled around one another to deliver "hello" kisses. When we settled into place, Tony was standing beside Elle, not me. Our positions formed the proverbial triangle; a part of my mind jeered in passing.

Tony and Elle were tripping over each other's words speculating for my benefit on the odds of first, she and Tony crossing paths, and now, running into me. They couldn't control their anxious prattle. I said a few polite words to show I was listening but, I wasn't; I was watching.

I watched as reality took shape before my eyes.

Not only were they standing beside each other, but they were so close their clothes were touching. Because they were talking animatedly, their bodies "accidentally" bumped into each other again and again, providing tiny lucky chances for physical contact.

I didn't need hawk vision to see the vibrant afterglow of a gratifying sweaty romp radiating from them. Their eyes sparkled. They couldn't stop making one-second eye contacts and, when their eyes met, I saw the physical jolt it triggered. They grinned stupidly and, as if a little drunk, couldn't avoid bubbling out silly giggles. They were overflowing with identical electric excitement. Their energies were perfectly in sync and they were buzzing at the same frequency.

They were so transparent, as obvious as if they wore bold-face posters around their necks saying "if you cannot prove it happened, it didn't happen; that's our story, and we're sticking to it."

I looked at her eyes, into their depths. She met my gaze without flinching. There was no trace of guilt there. She had taken what she wanted. It had been available for the picking. It was nothing personal.

I noticed I was cramping their style; they were getting antsy. I knew that the veil I'd drawn over the emotions raging beneath my calm exterior was threatening to fall away. I put the three of us out of our misery and casually explained I was in a hurry. We went through the motions of kissing "goodbye" and I left. Coincidentally, the two of them were going the same way ...

I walked off quickly. As soon as I was sure that I was safely alone I found an isolated place to sit. The term "meltdown" doesn't begin to describe how intensely I fell apart. A landslide of pain swept me over. "How many times can a person die?" I asked myself. Overwhelmed with grief, I couldn't stop crying anguished tears. I kept repeating to myself: "not Elle, not Elle, not Elle ..."

I had a long history of feeling wronged by people who supposedly loved me, but I was appalled by the cruelty of this blow. Elle! Even in my worst nightmares I hadn't dreamed it could happen.

I would be lying if I said I hadn't noticed the little electrical sparks flying between Tony and Elle, the stolen flirtatious smiles, the way they casually gravitated toward each other to be physically close, even for a brief moment, how they laughed a little too quickly at each other's jokes. I had seen everything; however, I had chalked it up to superficial attraction.

After all, she was gorgeous. Any man with a drop of red blood in their veins would be physically attracted to Elle. She knew she was beautiful and was aware of her feminine power. I remembered a male acquaintance of mine once commenting that she was a tease. Because I loved her, I had been offended by the slur. However, he had pegged her. She acted like that with all men, including Tony.

In my gullibility, because of how I was linked to Elle, I was sure that neither she nor Tony would cross that line. "Think again," I said to myself with a hollow laugh.

Once more, I had been blindsided. Being played for a fool was my forte.

When I got home Tony was already there. I didn't have to look into a mirror to know that my eyes were swollen from all the crying. Glancing over his newspaper, he eyed me briefly, but said nothing. His expression was cold and mean. His eyes said: "bottle it up and spare me the theatrics."

The moment stretched out. I stood rooted to the spot.

Because I hadn't moved, he cut a quick glance toward me. He made a production of taking a long drag from his cigarette and tapping the ash into the ashtray. It didn't take a mind-reader to see that he was using the time to decide which card to play next.

He pulled the Intimidation card. Carefully avoiding eye contact, he gave me a scalding once-over. He smiled, but it wasn't a genuine smile; it was a triumphant sneer meant to strip me of all dignity. I flinched. For good measure, he cast a warning glance. It meant "don't-go-there," and to signal that it was high time I got out of his face, he rattled his newspaper in annoyance, snapped it open wider, and raised it so that he disappeared behind it. Catching his dismissal, I moved along.

I could have confronted Tony, but I knew it was pointless. He would have denied any wrongdoing, laughed in my face, and told me my thinking was skewed, especially that I would be implicating Elle. We had been on that merry-go-round countless times before. Tony's position was always the same: "I will never come clean. You will never get an apology out of me. I will always come out on top."

As on every occasion, I would be left holding the bag and humiliated.

I can't take it anymore I thought: I'm leaving him.

If you decide to leave him, I'm there for you, said the voice of the Shrewd Force.

Trust yourself, she added.

Your self-respect is in the balance, she pointed out.

The self-respect comment hit a nerve. I felt compelled to seize the gauntlet and rise to the occasion.

Watch me! I shot back to her emboldened.

In my mind's eye, I saw myself striding back to the living room and telling Tony:

"that's it; I'm leaving you."

The power of those words moved me deeply and invigorated me. A wave of pride washed over me, leaving me renewed, my dignity restored.

Then, without warning, everything capsized. The inspiring vision I'd had disappeared. Dread slammed into me with the force of a freight train and I broke into a cold sweat as I realized, if I left, everyone would eventually know that Tony had slept with Elle.

In Technicolor, High-Definition and with poignant background sound effects, detailed images and multiple scenes of the public derision, judgement and ridicule I would face came to life on the screen of my mind's eye. The spectacle took me to a place of abject fear. I knew my self-confidence could not withstand that much humiliation. My soul had taken too many blows.

Fear prevailed over judgement.

Shoulders sagging, defeated, stripped of all dignity, I took the well-worn path of the coward and chose to live in shame. I bore my pain in silence and decided to continue living with Tony. I hated myself for making that choice but old habits die hard.

Lying in bed that night, while Tony slept soundly, my mind reviewed the day's events. Life had knocked me flat before but this time disillusionment ate away at my very soul. Curled in the fetal position I cried silently. I felt the presence of the Compassionate Force, but I was so consumed by pain that her gentle ministrations had no effect. The bleakness I felt was boundless and absolute. I heard a bone snap. It was my backbone.

I was traumatized.

The following morning, in the cold light of day, reality set in. I had two recalcitrant children to take care of, laundry and cooking to do, the overwhelming amount of work a Master's degree studies entailed, and a part-time job. There is no rest for the weary.

I had no one to talk to; no one to share the grief.

A short time later I developed an acute rash on the palms of my hands; they were so raw they bled for days. My anxiety also opened a hole in my stomach and I writhed in debilitating pain for weeks. I had developed stomach ulcers and they were always triggered by the stress of Tony's infidelities. From that point onward the ulcers got much worse.

Once again, I was overcome by the feeling of betrayal. And once again, I pretended I was all right because I was scared; I didn't realize that each instance had given me an opportunity to learn important life lessons. I had dealt with the pain of my relationship by sweeping things under the rug instead of trying to understand events and learn their inherent truths.

I wasn't a moron. I was aware that, by avoiding the lessons I was undermining myself; in spite of that knowledge, I had always chosen to stay. How was I going to face myself from this day forward?

I'd made my choice to stay with him; I had no right to complain.

I didn't have to take deep introspection to know that my relationship with Tony was beyond unhealthy; it was destroying me. Clearly, I didn't meet his needs and he surely didn't meet mine. So, why couldn't I let go? Why did I keep walking in circles? Why was I stuck in the same situations, tripping over the same problems?

Something needed to change, but I feared learning the lesson.

For months I went about my daily activities like a ghost, in a fog of defeat, disdain and self-loathing.

Life went on.

Chapter 10: The Pilgrimage

At thirty-nine, still hoping to save my marriage, I began a frantic search for "how to mend a broken relationship." Despite knowing for twenty-two years that my marriage was a sham, I still clung to "there must be a way to fix this." Some of us are really slow and I must be among the slowest. Never underestimate the power of auto-suggestion, especially when all the suggestions stem from self-loathing. I had become an expert at self-delusion.

I read a pile of self-help books on "how to save a marriage." All of them noted that "it takes two to tango," which was infuriating because, I felt that my case was different. I was the one who endured all the hardships and through thick and thin, had held on to this marriage. I had been a good wife. I was the injured party, here. I was the victim! Why hadn't anyone written about how to fix him?

One book emphasized doing some soul-searching to identify the blockages in one's life path. In desperation, I followed that advice. I had always been a good student. I applied myself and did the homework.

I followed the step-by-step instructions and, to my utter surprise, the exploration led me straight to the little box I had sealed tightly and dropped to the bottom of an imaginary deep dark well many years before. The little box was supposed to have sunk without leaving a trace. Apparently, it hadn't sunk deep enough.

It was all coming back to me. The little box contained the trauma of what had happened thirty-three years earlier to 6-year-old-me, Ti-Chérie. I didn't like dredging things up. I was scared. But I realized on some level that the little box had something to tell me; I went deep inside myself, asked for help and summoned the courage to follow through with the process.

That's our cue, said Lapis tugging at Lana's sleeve.

She's ready to deal with Ti-Chérie. Let's help her heal Ti-Chérie.

Lana and Lapis recognized this was a life altering moment. They understood as well that the time had come for them to join forces and act as one. In deference for the significance of the occasion, they collected themselves and stood face to face, hands tightly linked, eyes locked in a penetrating gaze.

This is what we came to accomplish, Lapis said.
Yes, it's our life purpose, Lana replied solemnly.

Lana and Lapis needed a plan. They were born to do this, so inspiration came easily. They decided to take Ti-Chérie on a pilgrimage. They chose to do the sacred walk of Saint James of Compostela.

Before setting out, Lana and Lapis went to the Ti-Chérie who had remained frozen in the front porch chair in Haiti all these years ago. They knelt to be at eye level with the little girl.

Hello, they said as one.

I'm Lana.

I'm Lapis.

We are the Forces that live within Chérie. She refers to us as the Compassionate Force and the Shrewd Force. We came to get you because it's time for you to heal. Will you come with us?

Ti-Chérie nodded yes. She had lost her speech on that fateful day.
In the presence of Ti-Chérie, Lana and Lapis did a short ceremony to set the intention for the pilgrimage. It would be a journey of

purification and for asking God to wash away all traces of fear and pain from the body, mind and soul of their Ti-Chérie.

Like pilgrims in search of healing had done since the Middle Ages, they took Ti-Chérie by the hand and began the journey. They walked the trail, stopping at every church, every chapel, every consecrated monument, and every hallowed place to pray for the recovery of their beloved child. The commitment Ti-Chérie displayed every step of the way was a testimony of how invested she was in the process.

As their pilgrimage progressed, several times Lana and Lapis thought they saw a glimmer of change in Ti-Chérie' eyes. They hoped that finally, their little girl would be healed and would recover her speech. But, each time, their optimism was short-lived as the flicker of vitality quickly vanished.

The grueling journey took months, but they never faltered and, step by step, prayer by prayer, they completed it. The Cathedral of Santiago de Compostela marks the end of the pilgrimage path and they were standing at its door. Filled with fervor and determination, Lana and Lapis held their wounded child tightly in their arms and stepped inside the church. They took Ti-Chérie to the crypt to experience the miraculous energy of the sacred relic of Saint James of Compostela.

For a long moment Lana and Lapis stood motionless, their eyes closed and their heads bowed in contemplation, Ti-Chérie tucked between them, close to their hearts. And then, they felt the little body wiggle slightly. Their eyes snapped open and they lifted Ti-Chérie's chin to search her face. What they saw was a revelation.

Ti Chérie's blank, lifeless stare from that first tragic day was replaced by a soft, crystal-clear gaze full of love and hope. The light radiating from her eyes was otherworldly. She wasn't smiling, but the lines of stress had faded away from her face and her features were relaxed.

Can you speak? Lana asked in earnest.

Sadly, Ti-Chérie lowered her eyes and shook her head "no."

It's all right, Lana and Lapis replied in perfect unison.

It will come, darling, Lana said.

This is a first step, Lapis added.

Lana reverently framed the face of her baby between her palms. Focused on the angelic gaze of Ti-Chérie, she said solemnly.

My sweetheart, you have been touched by the grace of Saint James of Compostela. It is done.

Ti-Chérie nodded.

To recover from the fatigue of the journey they decided to remain in the city for an extra day. The following morning, they went for a stroll, enjoying the beautiful streetscapes when the sound of a bell ringing insistently caught the attention of Ti-Chérie. Seeing her reaction, Lana and Lapis realized it was a sign. Quickly they asked a passerby where the sound was coming from and were directed to a nearby convent. They followed the entrancing sound.

When they arrived at the convent, they saw that it was a walled complex. They rang the door bell and, without hesitation, the nuns invited them inside. While Lana and Lapis told the nuns about their spiritual journey Ti-Chérie sat quietly in Lana's lap.

The convent was built around an inner courtyard with a garden at its center. From where they were sitting, they had an unobstructed view of large rectangular raised beds filled with almost ethereal flowers in exquisite colours. The garden could have come directly from heaven.

A young novice was sitting on the low wall of a flower bed. In total amazement, Lana and Lapis watched Ti-Chérie leave the safety of Lana's lap to walk purposefully toward the novice. As Ti-Chérie approached, the novice made eye contact with Lana and Lapis, silently asking permission to engage with the little girl. Lana and Lapis nodded as one to express their assent.

The novice crouched to be at eye level with Ti-Chérie and smiled warmly. Silently, they looked at each other for a long moment; the novice opened her arms and Ti-Chérie stepped into her embrace. The connection between them was complete. They looked like two souls who had known each other since the beginning of time.

The novice stood and extended her hand, silently inviting Ti-Chérie to come with her. With all the trust in the world, Ti-Chérie rested her tiny hand in the offered palm and they walked away together. One of the nuns turned to Lana and Lapis and simply said:

Our young novice is special.

When the pair returned to the courtyard a short while later, Ti-Chérie had been washed and groomed. Their baby radiated peace.

The transformation they witnessed was astounding. But despite the progress, Lapis knew that, even if she recovered completely, Ti-Chérie would always remain fragile and would never be able to cope with the cruelty of the outside world. It was clear to her that Ti-Chérie should remain in the convent which offered the protection she needed. She knew that Lana would be crushed at the idea of leaving Ti-Chérie behind and braced herself for an onslaught as she turned to Lana and said:

We need to talk.

The conversation was indeed difficult, but asking Lana to look at things from another perspective and with an open heart helped her understand and accept that leaving Ti-Chérie in the convent was for the best. Turning to Lapis, Lana said,

The pain of this separation feels as if I'm being skinned alive.

But, for the welfare of her child, she would do anything, including letting go. Gathering all her courage, with a resolve born of love, she said to Lapis:

Let's go talk with Ti-Chérie.

Ti-Chérie was sitting beside the novice, hand in hand. They had become inseparable. Lana broached the subject head-on. She explained how she and Lapis saw things and asked Ti-Chérie if she would agree to remain in the convent, without them. Lapis clarified that, as much as they would have liked to stay with her, they had to go back, Chérie needed them. The little girl looked into the eyes of the novice then turned to face Lana and Lapis. With a serene expression she nodded with conviction to say that she understood they had to leave and her choice was to remain at the convent.

Lana and Lapis were in awe. Their Ti-Chérie was transformed. They marveled at her resilience. Leaving Ti-Chérie was a painful decision and, despite her resolve, Lana was heart-broken. But it was for the best. At the convent Ti-Chérie would be safe and loved.

As Lana and Lapis walked to the door of the convent to leave, Ti-Chérie said *stop* in a firm, clear voice.

Shocked, Lana and Lapis froze for a second and then turned and ran to their little girl.

You can speak, you can speak, you can speak! Lana repeated astonished.

Lapis stared, tongue-tied. Lana, always the effusive one, knelt, wrapped her arms around her baby, rocked the small body and covered her little miracle-girl with kisses, repeating *you can speak* like a litany of thanksgiving.

Giggling, Ti-Chérie returned Lana's loving touches with affection and effusiveness. Ti-Chérie's giggles were the most beautiful sound in the world. When the intense outpouring of love subsided Ti-Chérie gave Lana a reassuring smile, a last small caress, and turning to Lapis, left Lana's embrace and stood.

With a reproachful expression she searched Lapis' gaze and spoke her mind.

Why didn't you help me when I needed you?

When I was screaming "I'm scared" inside my head, all you did was to tell me to be quiet. And after that, you disappeared.

Why? Why?

Lana couldn't believe her eyes. For the first time since she had known Lapis, she saw a wave of raw emotions sweep over her face: pain, shame, regret, guilt, anguish, fear and more. Even Ti-Chérie was surprised. Lapis had never, ever expressed emotions of any kind.

Ti-Chérie's accusation was devastating. Lapis looked ravaged.

Slowly, Lapis knelt not just to be at Ti-Chérie's level. It was a posture of repentance.

Lapis collected herself. Then, she faced Ti-Chérie and said:

On that fateful day I said what I did because I knew that, in life, some things are written. They must happen. There is no escaping.

I didn't have the power to change your fate.

I did what I thought was best under the circumstances: I provided a strong voice for you to latch onto. Had you screamed and made a scene on that day, you would only have complicated an already terrible situation.

Ti-Chérie considered this and recognized the truth of what Lapis had said. Making a scene would have exposed the actions of the man and the wrath of her father and the punishment he would have delivered would have known no bounds.

She recalled realizing that at the time and not wanting the consequences of that retribution on her conscience. With a nod, Ti-Chérie acknowledged she understood and some of the reproach left her eyes.

Appreciating the opportunity to continue, Lapis added:

As for disappearing, when you stopped hearing my voice it was because I had gone deep inside you, concentrating all the strength I could gather into holding your little heart with my bare hands, to give it the energy to continue beating.

I held your heart until I was sure it could continue beating by itself.

Looking inward, Ti-Chérie scanned and revisited her memories. Examining the terrifying events in light of what Lapis had said, she realized that, they did happen as Lapis described. She remembered her heart had indeed faltered but a force inside her had steadied it and then helped her through the practical motions of washing herself. She even remembered that it was Lapis who had told her to pick up a doll and hold it against her so as not to attract attention.

It all came flooding back.

The first time it happened was with the older man. He came to the house once a week to tidy the gardens. That day, I was on the back porch and he called me. Unsuspecting, I skipped my way towards him. But, as soon as he held my hand, I knew something was wrong; his grip was too tight. I panicked but didn't know what to do. Inside my head I started screaming, *I'm scared.*

A firm voice answered, *be quiet.*

He took me behind the maids' quarters. By that time every bone in my little body was shaking. I felt sheer terror and was transfixed by a debilitating fear. After he finished, he wiped me down crudely and, with a jerk of his head told me to leave.

An unknown force helped me put one foot in front of the other and go back inside the house; it told me to wash and change my clothes. I remember wanting to go curl up in my bed. But the voice directed me to pick up a doll and to go sit on the front porch in plain view. I followed those instructions and hitching my little body into one of the oversized wood lounge chairs, sat frozen like a statue, staring at nothing.

When my parents arrived home that night, they found me in the chair. At that moment I spilt in two: one of me remained frozen in the chair; the other greeted my parents with a smile, as usual. The one that went on living was subdued that night but, no one noticed.

Lapis had never failed her. On the contrary, Lapis had saved her. She had remained with Ti-Chérie while her life hung in the balance. Lana had attended to the other 6-year-old, the one who went on living as if nothing had happened.

All the sorrows of Ti-Chérie and of Lapis lifted. Both were restored.

Lana and Lapis didn't leave the convent that day. They spent hours with Ti-Chérie sorting through memories and comparing notes about how they had lived the moments, offering explanations and exchanging points of view.

They talked about how, by finding the inner strength to confront Lapis, Ti-Chérie had conquered her worst fears and unlocked the energy to live her life positively from this point forward and how Lapis too was freed and exonerated of any blame.

When all had been said, it was time for Lana and Lapis to leave. Their goodbyes were bittersweet.

Standing outside, the convent door, a hand on her hip, one eyebrow raised and her head tilted back appraisingly, Lana said to Lapis,

I still can't believe it; you have emotions!

A shy smile illuminated the face of Lapis. The emotion of the smile reached her eyes.
Smiling Lapis was a sight to behold.
The smile broke Lana's heart.

I'm sorry for the harsh things I said to you at times because you never expressed emotions outwardly, she said.

Once, I called you Vulcan.

In your place, I would have said much worse, said Lapis gesturing with her hand to say "all that was water under the bridge."

Now, I want to hear you laugh, Lana said.

Don't get ahead of yourself, countered Lapis with her usual serious face.

I believe in miracles, said Lana with a conviction that made Lapis do a double-take. The corner of Lapis' mouth twitched.

In a motion that came as naturally as if she had done it every day of her life, Lana put her arm around her sister's waist and held her tight. Driven by a need for connection that was totally new to her, Lapis locked the connection by draping her arm over her sister's shoulder.

Reveling in their newly found bond and walking in step, they headed for home.

Chapter 11: The Proverbial Straw

The kids, Tony and I had gone on vacation for Spring Break and were heading back home. It was well before dawn and we were preparing to leave for the airport. As is often the case in those moments, we were scrambling. That morning Tony woke up twitchy; every little thing got on his nerves. One of us couldn't find this or that item, the other one was taking too long in the bathroom, and the cat had disappeared.

This cat could read us so well that, without fail, the night before we travelled, he would go hide because he hated getting into the cage. The four of us were left searching every nook and cranny to find him. Tony wouldn't stop complaining. He was getting on my nerves so, I snapped back:

Make yourself useful instead of grumbling.

By the time we were in the taxi Tony was belligerent. When we stepped out at the airport, in what was supposed to look like a "spur-of-the-moment" decision, he raised one eyebrow to the maximum for effect, and, in a tone of finality, announced to me and the kids that he was divorcing me.

The children were genuinely surprised, but the real surprise came when Tony saw the expression of pure delight on my face; I was grinning from ear to ear! He was totally shocked and stopped dead in his tracks with his mouth open. His bewildered look said: "what did I miss." Clearly, he had expected me to fall apart.

I saw the Shrewd Force materialize before my eyes. I watched her approach Tony and lean in to whisper in his ear:

Think again.

Then she turned toward me and gave me a firm nod: "you've got this, girl!"

The Compassionate Force materialized as well. She was beaming with pride and overjoyed that I could see her. She wrapped me in her arms and said in a low voice:

You made it my darling!

While Tony checked us in with the airline, I became acquainted with my two forces. Ti-Chérie had met them for the pilgrimage. But, as an adult, it was the first time I was meeting them face to face.

The compassionate force introduced herself first.

Do you remember us? I am Lana, she said.

It means "precious and valued." I am fiercely nurturing by nature, the classic mother-hen. My area of expertise is emotions and interactions.

The other figure stepped forward and said":

You refer to me as the "Shrewd Force." It's an apt description. I am Lapis, the decisive one. I am guided by logic. I am practical, organized and efficient. My specialty is enhanced awareness and strength. I'm the problem solver. Lana here provides emotional support.

Her gaze bored into the depths of my eyes and said:

Don't be scared - we're with you.

Framed by Lana and Lapis I was filled with courage and determination. My day had finally come. After check-in we went for breakfast. I was in a buoyant mood, floating like a soap bubble. I was so happy; my feet didn't touch the ground! I had the children in stitches with jokes. To Tony's annoyance, I couldn't stop grinning; my effervescence grated on his nerves.

Lapis was enjoying the scene. She watched Tony unravel and whispered in his ear:

You didn't see that one coming, did you? Well, my friend, the bell has tolled for you.

As soon as we got home, I pulled Tony aside and said:

Regarding what you said earlier, that you want a divorce, I agree. As soon as I get back to the office this afternoon, I'll start looking for an apartment.

Fine with me, he replied feigning indifference. I could see right through his bluff and he knew it.

So many times, I had imagined telling Tony I'm leaving him. Not in my wildest dreams had I imagined that he would serve up my freedom on a silver platter. Life is full of surprises!

It may have been vindictive of me, but I couldn't resist; that night for supper I cooked his favorite meal and was unusually vivacious at the table. Taking in the food and my cheerful mood, Tony knew he was being laughed at. In the background, for my benefit, Lana and Lapis were doing a "you go, Girl" cheerleader routine with jumps, tumbling, and pompoms to the beat of power music.

Later that night, when we had settled in our respective corners of the house, I took the time to get to know Lana and Lapis better. They looked exactly like me. To an outside observer we looked identical; but our individual perspectives showed us the differences that made each of us unique.

For example, Lapis' gaze is laser-sharp. Only someone with a very strong back bone and inner force can hold that gaze. Lana's smile is so beautiful it would make an angel blush in delight. As for me, I could see in myself character traces of both; what differentiated me from them was my negative energy. They vibrated at a very high frequency; I vibrated at a low frequency.

Lana described herself as the Cancer energy in my astrological chart. Lapis as the Capricorn energy. They revealed that they weren't always the "dynamic duo" that they are now; in the past, they operated separately, supporting me with their respective forces. The change occurred when I decided to heal 6-year-old Chérie.

I wanted to know more about them and they obliged.

*Madame Lapis here,*Lana said, pointing to Lapis with a snappy side shake of head, *used to live behind a glass wall.*

My head swiveled to Lapis, my face puzzled. Lapis lifted her hands, palms facing outward in a gesture that said: "don't judge me too fast."

I'm a Capricorn, she explained,

So my middle name is control. One thing Capricorns love to control is their space. I put up the glass wall to secure my space. Looking back, I see that it may have been a tad drastic. However, in my defense, in those days, I wasn't exactly into girl-bonding.

No, no, no, no, said Lana to me.

I don't want you to get the wrong impression. I respect a person's need for space. The glass wall is not the crux of the matter here, Lana said shaking her head vigorously.

The issue is, and she shifted her body closer to mine to make sure she had my undivided attention, raised her voice slightly for better effect and leaned into each of the words that followed:

Lapis can walk right through that glass wall.

Lana held my gaze with a look that said: *try imagining that!*
I stared at Lapis in amazement. She ducked her head slightly and grinned.

You can walk through walls? I asked puzzled.

Lapis giggled shyly, like a little girl. At that sound, Lana did a double take. She was still mesmerized every time Lapis expressed emotions!

Let me tell you, Lana said tapping my forearm insistently.

Every time Lapis wanted to put on airs she would take a step filled with purpose and, as if nothing, pass right through the glass wall.

Trust me, she continued, *I've seen her do it many times. No matter how often she does it, it never gets old. Even today, I am mystified!*

I have to confess, Lana continued, *every time she did it I would surreptitiously move close to the wall and discreetly extend my hand to see if it would pass through the glass. Nope! How the heck does she do it?*

Lana's eyes shifted back and forth between Lapis and me with a questioning look.

I heard talk about people raising the vibration of their bodies. Is that how you do it, Lapis?

Lana turned imploring eyes toward Lapis with a quick glance in my direction, clearly hoping that Lapis would agree to disclose the secret for my benefit.

Ah! Lapis said, eyebrows and palms raised, shaking her head lightly to indicate "no point probing or capitalizing on Chérie's presence, I'm not revealing anything."

A girl has her secrets, she said in a case-closed tone.

I agree that my pass-through-the-glass trick has flair, she said with a touch of smugness.

However, Chérie, the Queen of Flair is Lana, she said, theatrically extending one hand toward her sister.

Invariably, Lapis continued, *to show me she can compete, Lana would, in one fluid move, dramatically lower her eyelids, slowly roll her eyes in my direction and point her nose up in the air to convey all the loftiness she can muster, pirouette on the ball of one foot and walk away with the grace of a prima ballerina.*

As if that wasn't enough, Lapis continued, *she would take things up a notch by making her dress trail behind in slow-motion waves, as if carried by a magical breeze. Trust me; the performance is a feast for the eyes. No matter how I try, I can't manage to pull off "regal". Only Lana can.*

Stretching her neck forward to better connect with Lana, Lapis asked, amusement dancing in her eyes,

Lana, how do you achieve the slow-motion dress-floating?

Lana lowered her head toward her left hand to examine her nails ...

They continued to entertain me with anecdotes for hours. I didn't sleep that night; I stayed up listening to their stories. I was beyond fascinated.

A couple of days later I informed Tony I had found an apartment and was moving out that very weekend.

You want to divorce? he said with a lilt that implied a question, as if he weren't the one who had demanded it, *fine, but, mark my words: you will never find another man.*

His words dripped rancor.

Tony had this pernicious habit of saying the harshest things to me just to watch me crumble. A few days later, with the demeanor of a prince, he would come back to the topic and say he hadn't meant the hurtful things he had said. He would say he had spoken them in anger.... But that was not an apology, and he had left scars ....

There was no doubt in my mind that he had hoped to rattle me by throwing divorce in my face. But this time his little game backfired. His spiteful words clearly indicated he didn't appreciate being the one left holding a lit firecracker.

In truth, Tony had taken the words about divorce right out of my mouth. I was ready. All the self-help books had borne fruit.

My point-of-no-return occurred on Valentine's Day.

In our area, Social Services always set-up hot lines for people who were alone or depressed on Valentine's Day. I saw the number advertised on television and jotted it down. It was after-hours and I rushed back to my work office to have some privacy. I dialed the number and a professional voice answered immediately.

I explained to him how, during the past twenty-three years, I had been chasing my tail in my marriage because of my husband's chronic infidelities. I recounted the number of times I had confronted him and how, every time, he had categorically denied any fault, using the same script:

My conscience is clear.
The issue is that:

> *you're an insecure woman;*
> *you have a burgeoning imagination; and*
> *you are hell-bent on self-destruction.*

I admitted that, every time he had thrown these words in my face, I had doubted myself. Except for one time, I hadn't caught him wrapped around another woman. Despite having first-hand witnessed all the blatant flirting and seducing, I was always riddled by the doubt - could there be a slim possibility that I was wrongly accusing him of adultery? The mental tug-of-war I went through drove me crazy.

After listening to me patiently the counselor asked:

> *Why do you put more trust in what he tells you? Why don't you trust yourself, your instincts?*

And there was light!

His simple words had pulled me out of the conundrum I had been stuck in for more than two decades. I thanked him from the bottom of my heart. I also said a prayer of thanks to the angel who had inspired me to make that call.

On the spot, my life changed. I trusted myself.

So, when a few weeks later Tony said he wanted a divorce, the news was music to my ears. Speculating on how timely his request was, I smiled and thought to myself; I guess someone is good at picking up vibes!

Moving out to live alone was not easy. 16-year-old-me couldn't stop wailing.

But I still love him she would scream at me.

For her, nothing could hurt more than losing her Tony. It was agony. Lana and Lapis considered 16-year-old and said:

We're going to have to keep a close watch on her. She could ruin all of Chérie's efforts.

Despite my determination to divorce, I could relate to 16-year-old. All she and I had ever wanted was to be happy with Tony. Influenced by 16-year-old, when I was alone, I cried a lot.

We have to keep close watch on both, said Lana.

Chapter 12: Taking Charge

In my experience, it takes about two years to adapt to a significant change like changing jobs, moving to a new city or separating after a long-term relationship. Two years is what it took for me to begin finding my footing after leaving Tony.

Sometimes, two years pass quickly. But sometimes they don't. After I left Tony, the days, weeks and months shifted as though my new reality was as congealed and thick as molasses. I was always on the run, but I didn't seem to get anywhere. Everything was stressful and required an enormous amount of effort.

I moved into my own place one week after Tony mentioned divorce. For convenience, I rented a furnished apartment, so all I had to haul were clothes, bed sheets, some tableware and pots and pans, plus all my CDs. The kids, who were now grown adolescents, helped me move. We started carting plastic bags early Saturday morning and before lunchtime, we were done.

The furnishings the apartment came with were basic and drab. So the afternoon of the day, instead of unpacking, I went shopping for things to decorate the place. I identify with the space I live in; to the point I feel it's an extension of me. It's not enough for my space to be just clean and well organized. It has to be aesthetically pleasing to my eyes.

So I knew that the first thing I had to do to settle in my new life was decorate the apartment. I have a good eye for form and color, and easily spotted what I would need to give the place character.

On Sunday morning, with all the purchases of the day before laid-out in front of me, I got working on dressing-up my new home. I made cushion covers with material from garments I had picked up at a thrift shop. I cut out photographs from an old calendar and mounted them on construction paper and cheap pieces of glass I got at the hardware store and, *voila*! The very weekend we moved-in, the place was transformed. It now felt like a home, like my home. Lana gave me a two-thumbs-up.

Later, while I was unpacking and cleaning, Lapis kept insisting on the importance of making a list of what needed to be done. Thank goodness for her practical mind - I don't know what I would have done without her.

> *I've got a draft checklist going,* Lapis said, *so that we don't forget anything.*

I briefly glanced at her. She had a pencil lodged behind her right ear; she was holding a small notepad; and her hair was pulled back and tied in a tight, no-nonsense bun. "Bless your heart" I mouthed to her! She closed her eyes and nodded slowly and silently to indicate "I'm here for you."

The apartment had one bedroom with two beds, so I gave that room to the children and created a space for myself in the entrance closet. It was just big enough to accommodate my yoga mat on the floor and a small night table at the foot of the mat. From a nearby electrical plug, I ran an extension cord and plugged-in a small lamp to illuminate my "room."

Above the nightstand I installed a thrift-shop corkboard. I knew that I was now in charge of every aspect of my life, so being well-organized was essential.

That first night, seated on my makeshift bed, I made my first list with the help of Lapis. On a calendar, I circled the days I would receive my paychecks. A few weeks later I added the due dates of my monthly bills and the birthdays I didn't want to forget.

From that point onward, my life was structured around my "to-do" list and reminder notes that included magazine articles and quotes I found inspiring.

During those first two years Lapis took charge. Together, we ran on pure Capricorn energy. It wasn't difficult for us to tap into that fuel source. According to my birth chart, my astrological sign is Capricorn; I have the Sun, the Moon, the North Node and Mercury in Capricorn.

Taking charge came as naturally to Lapis and me as breathing. With clear intent Lapis and I harnessed our innate down-to-earth practicality and rigorous discipline, charged it with focus, and funneled the resulting energy into tackling lists.

First, I had to find a second job. Although, as architect, I had a decent salary, it wasn't enough with the added expense of the apartment. Secondly, I needed a lawyer to work on my divorce - another disbursement. The last details included administrative tasks like contacting utility companies and notifying institutions and agencies like Health Care, Department of Motor Vehicles, Banks, etc. of my new contact information.

Within a couple of days, I had a part-time job. The Saturday following my move I began work as a cashier at a nearby general store. My professional life included full days Monday to Friday. From 6:00 to 9:00 on weekday evenings and 9:00 am to 6:00 pm Saturdays and Sundays, I did my cashier job, earning minimum wage; so I needed both the evening and weekend shifts to supplement my income.

Holding two jobs and taking care of the kids defined my day-to-day routine. I was perpetually swamped. My day at the office ended at 5:00 pm. I would rush home, swallow something, then rush to the store for my evening shift. When I returned home after 9, I had to clean, do laundry, and cook so that the children would have prepared meals for lunch and supper every day.

Taking-charge energy is potent; however, it is also raw, particularly when you're a woman. There is nothing soft about it. It doesn't induce laughter, smiles or sentimentality. It means business, cutting to the chase, and no foolishness. It can be overwhelming, especially if you also have a soft and affectionate side.

Added to the fact that I barely had time to breathe, 16-year-old had decided to be rebellious, and didn't allow me a moment's peace. At all hours of the day and night her wailing would fill my head, threatening my sanity. It was like having an aggressive animal constantly circling me, growling and occasionally snatching a bite. Because of her, I lived in emotional high-alert.

Lana tried every way she knew to console 16-year-old but nothing worked. 16-year-old was full of anger and wouldn't be soothed. Her resentment knew no bounds. She was a mutinous teenager who wouldn't stop acting-out until what had been taken away from her was restored: her Tony. She was spoiling for a fight and determined to find one. She wore me down.

The worst times were at night. During those quiet moments, overcome by fatigue, I would let my guard down. Unprotected, I would be overwhelmed by the emotions of 16-year-old and felt her pain, confusion and broken-heartedness. When her emotions and mine merged this way, she would stare at me with hate-filled eyes and say:

You like feeling that way? That's where you've boxed me!

Most of all, it was her loneliness that crushed me and I would end up crying myself to sleep.

The following morning Lapis would breathe enough energy into me to get me up and together, we would force ourselves through our routine. Emotionally, each day felt like an eternity.

But despite the physical and emotional hardships, I didn't miss a single day of work on account of the separation.

About six months into my new life, realising I was reaching the end of my rope and always addressing the practical side of things, Lapis called a Council of War. It excluded 16-year-old. How Lapis managed to keep 16-year-old away I don't know and, in truth, didn't care. I was just grateful to have a break from her complaining.

Lapis chaired the meeting. First order of business was finding ways to keep me from spiraling into depression. According to Lapis, it was important to keep my mind occupied. I loved to read; therefore, Lana suggested romance novels.

The novels won't require intellectual effort, she noted.

Good, I said, *because I have none to spare.*

Lapis mentioned a brain wave machine she had seen advertised on television. The device came in the shape of shielded goggles that emitted pulsating light which put your brain into Alpha or Theta mode. I seconded the idea with enthusiasm. I love technological gadgets!

Lana raised the idea of prayer. She acknowledged that I prayed every day and commended me for it.

However, she noted, *your prayers are supplications.*

Instead, she suggested, *create a sacred place from which to connect with the Divine. No more lamenting.*

I'll teach you how to do it and we'll do it together, she promised.

Thank you, I said gratefully.

The next point of discussion was 16-year-old. I couldn't keep myself from rolling my eyes in annoyance. Lapis pretended not to see, and let it slide.

I don't have the power to make her disappear, Lapis said to me.

The best I can do, for as long as you need, is shield you from her ranting. She will still be there, but I'll lower her volume ...

Curiosity got the better of me; I had to ask:

What did you do with her?

She's behind my glass wall, answered Lapis with the hint of a smile stretching one corner her lips.

Before moving-on from the topic of 16-year-old Lana looked at me seriously and said:

You do understand that, one day, in the foreseeable future, you will have to deal with 16-year-old, don't you? One: she cannot remain permanently behind the glass wall. Two: only you have the power to deal with her.

I understand, I said.

But, for now, I pleaded, *I need all my strength just to put one foot in front of the other each day.*

Lana and Lapis exchanged a look, then turned to me and nodded in understanding.

Don't worry, Lana added, *16-year-old won't be alone; I'll take care of her.*

In closing, we discussed my physical exhaustion. Lapis came closer to me, until our noses almost touched. She held my face between her open palms, bored her eyes into mine and said.

I know you're worn-out, but you can do it. Trust me, you can do it. I'll hold you.

16-year-old having been muzzled; I could relax a bit. At night, to the sound of my favorite songs I read romance novels back-to-back like a chain smoker. I spent time in my sacred place every day and routinely used my special goggles to coax my brainwaves into good frequencies.

Things became bearable.

The lawyer I hired to help with my divorce had explained that the simplest approach was to petition for divorce after living apart for twelve consecutive months. As soon as the waiting period ended, I filed for divorce and it was granted.

Holding the divorce papers in my hand made me feel, for the first time since the separation, that I had actually achieved something tangible. While I recognized it was an achievement, at the time, more than anything, it represented my failure at life. Looking at the written proof of my divorce, my practical mind asked: what's the next step?

Next, I thought matter-of-factly: change your name. Back in the day, when I got married, women were required to take the names of their husbands. However, thinking and custom had evolved. I initiated the process to reinstate my maiden's name.

The name-change entailed lengthy administrative procedures to update all ID cards, official documents, contact information with service companies, credit cards, insurance etc. Muddling through the process left me drained. When it was finally done, the thought of celebrating the name reversal never crossed my mind.

Just a few months later I had my gall bladder removed because it was chock-full of big stones. It would take years before the divorce and name-change made me feel free.

For economic reasons, Lapis and I kicked around the idea of buying a house. We saved every penny we could and a bit more than one year after the divorce we had the deposit for a cheap little fixer-upper. The deterioration of the house was so extensive it had been boarded for a couple of years.

This is our house, said Lapis with the confidence of someone who has second sight.

Work doesn't scare us!

Despite Lapis' determination, I worried about biting off more than I can chew. To dispel my fears, she made me laugh. With the panache of a self-assured cowboy hero fastening-on his gun-belt, Lapis hitched an impressive tool belt to her hip, stood legs apart in a power-posture and gave me a crooked smile. Wide-eyed, cocking her head while pointing a thumb in the general direction of Lapis, Lana asked quizzically:

Since when does her repertoire include showing-off?

I took the plunge.

I told my work colleagues that I had bought an obsolete house. Much to my surprise, a couple of engineers I was close to immediately offered to help with the repairs. For a nominal fee, in their free time, they upgraded the electrical system and the plumbing, ordered and installed new windows, changed the roofing and tore down one interior wall!

A female co-worker from Finance volunteered to handle flooring.

My flooring-installation skills are second to none, she said, brimming with self-confidence while sitting in a cubicle bursting at the seams with Himalayan-high piles of invoices and financial printouts. In my mind I tried to reconcile the accountant/handy-woman combo. As it turns out, she was jaw-droppingly excellent with flooring.

Two good friends, who knew I had a bad back and was still dragging from fatigue following surgery, took care of painting the exterior of the house. They did it for free! I had purchased enough paint for two coats. They purchased more paint for a third coat out their own pockets.

At the office, my little house was the main topic during coffee breaks. Everyone wanted details on how the work was progressing. The two engineers and my Finance co-worker were regularly showered with high praise for their generosity, skills and efforts.

The run-down shack was transformed into a precious little bungalow. It was the pride of my co-workers and friends. The good vibrations emanating from that little house transformed me as well. They brought hope to my life.

I realized the little house was a beautiful reward and I was grateful. This motivated me to seek positive transformation in other aspects of my life. What I wanted most was to become a better person, the best I could be. With that mindset, I felt encouraged to work more on myself. Among other things, I focused on goals like not letting my hard feelings towards Tony fester into hate.

It had taken about two years to reach this turning point.

Chapter 13: The Relapse

WHAT was I thinking???

"Fool me once, shame on you; fool me twice, shame on me."

The little house was a moment marked with pride. It was my beacon of hope. With the little house something shifted; it was tangible proof of my accomplishment. I began to trust.

Living in my little house was a joy. My spirits lifted. When the renovations were completed, I stopped working night shifts and only worked weekends. Not having to work evenings improved my quality of life tenfold.

About two years after getting the little house I had surgery for stomach ulcers. All these years, I had lived with chronic and sometimes excruciating pain. There hadn't been a single day free of pain. A few days after the surgery the children and I went to a lovely tropical island. It was Christmas.

Out of the blue, a few days into our vacation Tony showed up. He knew where we were; I'd given him the details because of the children. He stayed at a separate hotel saying he knew I wasn't well and simply wanted to spend Christmas with us.

He didn't pressure me. Instead, he treated me as if I was just a relative, and only stayed three days. Going to the beach, eating together, taking long lazy strolls felt like being a family again. I could see the children were happy.

When the children and I returned, Tony kept in touch. He wooed me very slowly, exactly like the first time. At first, he just called to inquire about my health. Then, occasionally, he would come and pick me up for a short outing such as going for ice cream. Slowly, we became reacquainted. He complimented me on my little house.

One day a few months later he took me on a car-picnic. He parked in an isolated area by the waterfront. The setting was beautiful; the light dancing off the surface of the water added a touch of magic. While we ate tasty sandwiches, he casually suggested we forget about the past and start anew.

We have a lot of unresolved issues, I pointed out. He submitted that the divorce had changed both of us; we were no longer the same people.

Dredging up past mistakes will not rewrite the past, he rationalized.

Instead of throwing our shortcomings at each other, let's leave the past in the past and begin a new life as brand-new people. We both know what we lost; we will be more careful this time around.

I fell for it hook, line and sinker.

Shortly after, he suggested we move in together, and I agreed. He bought a new house to symbolize our fresh start. I felt reassured about his good intentions. To reciprocate, I rented out my little house and moved in with him. We were a family again.

About nine months later I began seeing signs of the old Tony. At first, he became distant and would keep me at arm's length as if to say "stop crowding me." Then flirtatious behaviour with other women began to take place in my presence.

We had planned to take a little vacation together in the islands, just the two of us. The hotel and the plane tickets had been purchased. But, when the time came to travel, he had all kinds of excuses for postponing the trip. Unsurprisingly, there was a woman in the background.

I went on the trip alone. I needed the space. I didn't get any.

While I sat on the beach mindlessly listening to waves lapping and staring into nothing, Lana and Lapis stood a few feet back, observing me. They were shoulder to shoulder, arms crossed, heads leaning inward toward each other.

She's lost, Lana said.

Lost her head is more like it, replied Lapis.

Unfortunately, continued Lapis, *it's going to get much worse before it gets better.*

Always up for a challenge, Lapis decided

Let me go see what I can do to help her find her bearings.

In that case, said Lana, *I will go to 16-year-old. She's probably having the tantrum of the century.*

Good-luck, they said to each other sarcastically, knowing that instead of luck, backbreaking work awaited them both.

Lapis pulled a chair in front of me, planted it firmly in the sand and sat so close our knees touched. She stared me down. I flinched; hard. I knew from the intensity of the stare that she wasn't going to give an inch. I was no match for angry Lapis and there was nowhere to run. I felt as though I were facing a firing squad.

Clearly, Lapis wasn't going to make things easy for me; she was waiting for me to speak first. With a shaky voice I started with what seemed like the obvious:

I know, I said sheepishly, *here I am, five years later, back at Square One.*

Tut, tut, tut, tut, tut, cut in Lapis rudely, shaking her head and waiving her index finger so close to my face my eyes crossed. Leaning in for effect, she added, *don't you dare think you're going to hide under the I'm-a-victim rock. And, if you intended to build on this back-to-Square-One statement you just blathered, with something like "I thought he meant what he said," I strongly suggest you swallow it.*

She didn't lean back; she remained too close to my face, her gaze boring straight into my soul.

I know it was stupid of me to fall for it, I pleaded, *but that's exactly what happened. He said all the right things and I fell for it.*

Lapis slightly cocked her head, to better appraise me, and said,

reaaallyyyy?

She dragged out the word until it was alive with sarcasm.

Okay, she said crossing her arms and leaning back.
You want to take the scenic route; let's do that.

Her leaning back didn't leave me feeling as if she'd given me some space. On the contrary, it felt as if the space between us was now a black hole, inexorably sucking in anything in its periphery. I felt like someone close to losing her footing while standing on the edge of a very dangerous vortex. "This doesn't bode well," I thought.

Teetering on the edge, I wondered whether the "I-need-to-pee" ploy would work. "Bad idea," I told myself nervously.

So, you believed him, Lapis continued, *explain to me how you came to think you could place your confidence in him. Give it to me step by step so that I can follow your thought process. I'm listening.*

I know, I know, I said floundering; *what was I thinking?*

No, you don't, Lapis snapped, in a tone as sharp as a whip.

What? Now you're doing a variation on the I'm-a-victim theme? You're doing the I'm-the-injured-party refrain; therefore, my afflicted heart needs soothing?

I don't do soothing.

What stupidity will you try next: I need to go pee?

Don't test me.

She must have taken Drama School classes on how to play "Ice Queen" a part of my mind surmised in passing.

You said you believed him; I'm listening.

Instinctively, I looked right and then left. The primitive human in me felt trapped by life-threatening danger. Lapis read me as if I were transparent and observed:

You're looking around; what are you looking for?
If it's Lana, she's busy with 16-year-old.

"Oops," I thought and quickly cast my eyes down, way down. "Let's not touch that can of worms," I warned myself.

Lapis remained silent until I raised my eyes back to hers, and she grinned slyly from ear to ear. "If a fox could grin, this is what it would look like," I thought.

Nobody is coming to save you.
It's you and me.
Chop, chop!

I knew what Lapis was getting at. She wanted me to identify why things went wrong but, for the life of me, I couldn't see the lesson. I wasn't trying to be obtuse; nothing came to mind, despite my good intentions.

A little voice coming from a far corner of my mind piped up and said:

I'd keep the "I'm feather-brained" excuse to myself if I were you.

Sound advice, I thought.

I don't know what to do, I said to the little voice in desperation.

Ask her for help, supplied the little voice.

Excellent tip. Thank you. When this is over, and if I survive, I will drop by to shake your hand.

I looked at Lapis and submitted:

The only thing I understand at this point, Lapis, is that I'm lost.
Please, I'm genuinely stuck; help me.

Her eyes blinked lightly as she nodded almost imperceptibly.

Just start from the beginning, she said calmly.

I went back to the day Tony came to the island and continued from there.

I was physically tired, emotional and vulnerable at the time, I recounted.

His presence caught me off guard. It stirred feelings in me. It made me realize I was tired of being alone. The familiarity of him felt good. The rest just happened; I don't know how.

Are you serious? Lapis said with exasperation.

In one coordinated movement, Lapis tilted her head back, looked up and raised both arms at an imaginary Heaven. I didn't have to be a mind reader to understand she was silently begging to be delivered from the responsibility of this dimwit (me). Her body language and dumbfounded expression practically screamed "What did I do in a past life to deserve this?"

Turning to me, she said:

You do realize, don't you, that your explanation is a mirror image of the classic excuse used by husbands who have affairs?

Typically, they say "it just happened; I don't know how."

No quarter for you, Chérie, I thought.

You asked for help. I am duty-bound to give it to you. However, let the record show it's without pleasure, Lapis declared.

To help you I will give you a hint.

I had a dreadful feeling about the proffered "help" and the distinct impression it was going to blow-up in my face. I had never had an anxiety attack before but, at that moment, I felt one coming on.

The husband who has an affair, enunciated Lapis:
decided to flirt with another woman;
decided to invite the other woman out for coffee and then supper;

decided to take the other woman to a secluded place to have sex; and

decided to deny everything if asked.

In case you didn't catch it, decided was the operative word in my analogy.

Let me help you out a tiny bit more, she said with a facial expression and little hand gesture that said: "this one is on the house."

I ask you to explain yourself; you hide behind the curtain of denial and talk nonsense.

If you're going to hide behind excuses and use the "it just happened" rationale, then, have the moral decency to go back to the chapter you entitled "The Deceit" and remove all those intentions you attributed to your mother's actions.

The way I see it, when it came to reading and fleshing-out her motives, you had insight in spades and your mind was as sharp as a tack. However, when it comes to reading yourself, you're incapable of firing two brain cells.

If you cannot shed the same bright light on your motives, go rewrite that chapter from the angle that "things just happened" and wash your mother clean of all her alleged faults.

Ouch! This was one of those moments when you're so filled with shame you wish the ground would open and swallow you. Lapis was taking no prisoners.

Lapis was on a roll.

I'll give you another nudge in the right direction, she said with a little nose-scrunch that could have looked cute. In this instance, however, the nose-scrunch conveyed cynicism, lots of it.

But, before we go any further, Lapis said

just to make sure we're on the same page, list for my benefit the reasons why you left Tony.

She said it in the tone of a teacher helping a child work through a math problem.

I supplied the following:

I left him because in our relationship:

I lived with doubt and uncertainty;

I felt neglected;

when I felt most vulnerable and looked to him for support, I felt left out in the cold;

I experienced disapproval and opposition;

I cried much, much more than I laughed.

Now that we're clear about how you experienced your relationship with Tony, if I follow your rationale, your justification for your behavior is that the person with whom you experienced what you describe above stirred feelings in you?

This person who prompted the feelings summarized in the five above noted statements STIRS feelings in you? She said with exaggerated bewilderment.

When you put it that way, I see your point, I said.

No, no, no, no, no, no, you don't see my point. Please, allow me to lead you to my point.

Lapis doesn't suffer fools gladly.

The above-mentioned person STIRRED you and, the following JUST HAPPENED:

He played family with you in an idyllic setting at Christmas time: you enjoyed it.

He called you up to chat and to ask how you were doing: you allowed it.

He invited you for fun little outings: you went along.

He flirted with you: you melted.

He said "let's forget about the past": excellent outlook, you thought, after all, the past isn't relevant; it's all about the NOW.

He said let's move-in and play house: you pulled out your prettiest apron and tied it on neatly.

If you feel I put a biased spin on things, go ahead, don't be shy, say it.

I cast my eyes down and bowed my head very low in shame.

Am I to understand you have nothing to offer in your defense? Lapis asked, *seething with frustration at my silence?*

I kept my head down and nodded.

If you think you're getting off the hook with your "I'm contrite" attitude, think again. I want answers.

While you're "thinking" I'll add one more point, continued Lapis.

Look at me, she said menacingly.

If looks could kill, I would have died.

Don't ever let me catch you rolling your eyes on account of 16-year-old again. She's 16, for goodness' sake. You, on the other hand, are forty-five and look at what you're up to.

Leave it to Lapis to cut you down to size.

We sat in silence and the moment stretched.

Lapis' ruthless logic had pushed me exactly in the direction she wanted me to go: in that dark place to face what was lurking in the shadows. Again, instinctively, I looked right and left but, the darkness was jet-black. I thought of running; however, the consequence would be deleting "The Deceit." Over my dead body am I deleting that chapter!

FOCUS, Chérie!

I sat in the darkness and waited. I knew if I waited long enough, something would come up. After what felt like an eternity, something came. I waited longer, until it was close enough, intense enough that I could identify it.

It was FEAR. With that knowledge, everything clicked into place. I opened my eyes, looked at Lapis and said:

I understand what happened to me.

She made a hand gesture that was an invitation to proceed.

When Tony joined me on the island at Christmas time, his presence made me feel vulnerable and triggered me. I didn't realize it then, but it triggered my worst fear: the fear of being alone for the rest of my life. The feelings he stirred were based in neither love nor affection. They stemmed from fear.

I have felt abandoned and rejected many times in my life. His presence reflected to me that I was alone. On some level, I associated him with his promise that I would never find another man. I got scared. I was scared, scared beyond measure of ending up alone for the rest of my life. Because I was scared, I latched onto him.

That initial fear set in motion a domino effect. Allowing the telephone calls, flirting, getting back together without addressing any of our issues were all motivated by fear.

Lapis got up, pulled me up from my chair and hugged me with the tenderness of the most loving mother.

Love of my life, she said softly, swaying both of us as you instinctively do when holding a baby.

You were never alone and you never will be.

Not having a partner and being alone are two, very different things. Remember, you were never more alone than when you were with a husband. Another person cannot fill the emptiness you refer to as "being alone." Only you can love yourself as you want to be loved.

Lana and Lapis met up.

How are things with Chérie? asked Lana.
She did well,' replied Lapis with motherly pride.
She took her first step on the path of healing. And you, with 16-year-old?
I think I made some headway. Please, remove her from behind the glass wall.

Taking satisfaction in the feeling of a job well done and brimming with pride, they congratulated each other: Lana extended her palm face up horizontally and Lapis slapped it energetically and with attitude.

Look at us, Lana said, *we're like a couple of teenagers.*
A bit more we'd be doing cartwheels, Lapis said and laughed with abandon.

Time stopped. To Lana, the sound of Lapis' peal of laughter felt like a religious experience.

You laughed, said Lana moved to tears.

The day after I returned from the Caribbean I packed and moved out, without giving Tony any explanation. He never asked why.

Chapter 14: Forgiveness

I've thought a lot about it and I have concluded that healing is one of the most difficult things to achieve in life. It requires relentless effort and, it's never done. It's exhausting.

In the novels I read, the young woman who decided to heal does it in no time at all. Within a year, tops, she frees herself of all the fears hanging like a millstone around her neck; lands either a new, much better job, or a fantastic promotion; moves to an apartment with good bones filled with magical light and furnishes it elegantly as the interiors you see in *House & Home*. That accomplished, and having repeated positive affirmations daily, she meets the Man of her Dreams.

My experience involved twenty years' work to make a noticeable difference in my life.

One night I dream of Ti-Chérie. She was in the Convent's courtyard garden. She took my hand and we strolled the paths between the flower beds. She said she could tell I felt discouraged. I admitted that, after leaving Tony for the second time, I had expected to feel better; instead, I again felt like a failure. Ti-Chérie told me I had to try to understand why I felt that way.

You have to heal, she said.

When I woke up the next morning, I resolved to take care of myself.

I looked at myself closely. My confidence was shattered; I was full of wounds; and I didn't know who I was, really. With this realization, I knew things had to change. I wanted to experience wholeness and wellness. I wanted to create a life that would allow the real, authentic me to emerge and flourish.

Diligently, I took inventory of my wounds; examining each one separately, I identified the special attention and the gentle care each one required.

The list included the little girl who had grown up without the tender love of a mother; the adolescent who had believed she was damaged goods; the young woman who had been ostracized by her family and humiliated by her husband; and, the middle-aged woman who had hated herself for being gutless and staying with a man who had never loved her. More recently, there was the woman ashamed of the relapse.

Looking over my shoulder, 16-year-old Chérie read my list and fell to the floor, weeping. She was devastated because it implied that Tony didn't love her. Her whimpers were those of a mortally wounded child. Affected by her pain, I felt lured by the denial she clung to.

Lana and Lapis stood on high alert.

16-year-old has to be dealt with! Clearly, she wasn't ready to leave the glass room, exclaimed Lapis upset.

This time, I'm taking care of her, declared Lapis firmly.

I'm going to make sure she strikes "sabotaging" from her vocabulary forever!

What are you going to do? asked Lana, worried by Lapis' aggressive demeanor.

I'm going to slap that moaning out of her. When I'm finished with her, she'll think twice about playing with people's feelings. Sometimes in life, a good spanking is what it takes.

In one swift move Lana stepped in front of Lapis and cut her off. They were nose to nose.

Hitting is not allowed, said Lana very, very firmly.

Since when? objected Lapis loudly, frozen in a belligerent stance and not at all fazed by Lana's toughness.

Since the last century, asserted Lana.

For example, in the early seventies, Sweden, an enlightened country, passed laws against corporal punishment.

Lapis deflated as quickly as a popped balloon. Not one to break rules, she immediately changed her mindset and was busy focusing on finding an alternative to spanking when Lana's movements caught her attention.

What are you doing? asked Lapis.

I'm rolling up my sleeves, replied Lana.

We're not allowed to hit, she continued, *'but we darn well are allowed to gang up on her. 16-year-old is jeopardizing Chérie's mental health. If this adolescent can't understand her responsibility to do right by Chérie, it is OUR responsibility to teach her how to do that. We have to help her, Lapis! Are you with me?*

What did you have in mind? asked Lapis, adding *I'm definitely in!*

I'm thinking of a Good-cop/Bad-cop routine, said Lana like an astute political tactician. *I'll play Good-cop,* she specified, smiling beatifically - the Virgin Mary had nothing on her...

On cue, Lapis zoned into "Ice-Queen" mode ... Robocop himself could have learned a thing or two from her.

Neither Lana nor Lapis never told me what was discussed that day, but since then 16-year-old has disappeared and the sobbing sounds are no more.

Relieved of 16-year-old's moaning I calmed down and got back to uncovering the important questions that plagued me.

The process took years, one small step at a time. Gradually, the questions surfaced; over time, I got answers that allowed me to move on.

- Why did they break me? It was to find Resilience, now my super power.
- Why weren't they there for me? So that I'd learn to stand on my own two feet and master the skill of being joyously independent when I'm alone.
- Why didn't they love me? Being deprived of their affection taught me to love myself fully and understand the reciprocity of real love.
- Why didn't they want to change? It was never about them; it was always about me learning to grow in strength and to change myself.
- Why did they lie to me? It was to test my resolve to live honestly.
- Why was I subjected to these soul-shattering experiences? Pain gave me the impetus to modify things in my life; it inspired change.

I was making good progress.

It had been years since the last incident with 16-year-old. I was already in my fifties when, one day, out of the blue, she popped up. Lana and Lapis materialized instantly and stood in front of me, forming an impenetrable shield.

I have things to say, announced my 16-year-old self standing ram-rod straight and speaking in an uncharacteristically firm voice.

Lapis eyed the young girl suspiciously. Filled with mistrust about where this was going but not wanting to act hastily, she deferred to Lana.

What are your thoughts?

Lana tilted her heard and did a one-eye squint that said "what is our 16-year-old up to?" Like Lapis, she had misgivings, and wondered whether they should risk it. But, guided as always by tender feelings, she quickly turned to Lapis and said,

We are committed to openness.

Lapis trusted Lana implicitly. She also knew, from personal experience, that a story often contains more than meets the eye or ear. With a quick, firm nod, she agreed that 16-year-old should be allowed to speak. Together, they turned and cast a questioning look my way. I consented with a slow blink, and they nodded to 16-year-old to indicate "we're listening."

16-year-old smiled to show she appreciated the opportunity; her eyes were full of gratitude. Composed, she began.

I know you take me for a self-centered brat and, I now see that opinion is well deserved. In my defense, she pleaded looking straight at me, *I lived through things differently than you.*

I admit, she argued, *that I cherry-picked what I chose to remember. But, please, understand, I am 16 years old, although, clearly, I'm an immature one – Ti Chérie is more mature than me.*

When you are sixteen, she resumed, *you fall in love with the little things. I found Tony's lisp a-d-o-o-o-rable. I was in awe when I watched him act all grown-up; although he was only nineteen, he could sit with adults and discuss world affairs with ease … and I loved his dance moves! I, on the other hand, was pathetically shy and had no self-esteem. I was vulnerable and, even if I couldn't admit it to myself, I wanted so much to have a second chance at life.*

With the simplicity and innocence of a girl who still believed in fairy tales, I fell head over heels in love. All I wanted was to create a future with Tony. My best memories of the "good times" during the marriage are when he was feeling affectionate and flirted with me. I fell for his charm every time. I'm a sucker for charm.

16-year-old paused and then conjured up my 18-year-old self. Addressing her, she submitted:

Selecting memories that only served me, I remembered how, in the beginning of your marriage, you and Tony were wildly in love and full of plans and dreams.

Now, I also remember what it was like to be 18 and shattered by the pain of feeling worthless.

Now, I also remember abandoning you because I didn't want to face problems. Please forgive me.

She called upon my 23-year-old self and said to her:

I remembered you bought a book about pregnancy and, each month, you and Tony would read the relevant chapter out loud. Those moments were so precious.

I remembered, during both pregnancies, Tony would sometimes drive across town to get you something you felt like eating. He was so, so kind in these moments.

Now, I also remember what it was like to be a young mother feeling totally alone.

She called-in my 30-year-old self.

I remembered it was with Tony that you discovered the book "Impersonal Life." That book marked a turning point in your spiritual search.

Now, I also remember what it was like to be thirty, clinging to a marriage in tatters in order to raise the children, and smiling through the pain every day.

She asked my 40-year-old self to appear.

I selfishly remembered we traveled to exotic places and enjoyed wonderful family vacations.

Now, I also remember what it was like to be forty, hopeless, resigned to loss, and with no plans.

Addressing me, 16-year-old said:

Now, at 50-something, you're alone and still struggling to put the pieces back together.

She looked at each of us one at a time – 18, 23, 30, 40-year-old and me.

Of all of us, she said with a sweeping gesture.

I'm the one stuck on Tony, she accused herself, striking her heart with her closed fist.

I'm the one who refused to let go.

I've been watching the work you have all been doing to reclaim your power. I've thought a lot and tried to understand why, unlike you, I resisted moving on. At long last, I think I know the answer: Looking back, if I remained stuck at denial it's because I didn't want to forgive. Forgiveness requires change; change demands effort. I wanted the easy way out. I wanted the problems to disappear without any effort on my part.

Realizing that the issue at stake was forgiveness gave me a jolt because I didn't feel up to the task.

Fortunately, the jolt was followed by a revelation: my particular responsibility in our story, she said, gesturing to include all of us, *was to learn the lesson of forgiveness.*

It took a while for everything to sink in. But I began to realize that learning to forgive was my life purpose. Still, the task was daunting. Clarity is one thing; taking action is another, and choosing the appropriate action is yet another.

I struggled with the concept of forgiveness because, for the longest time, I was convinced it was Tony I had to forgive. It took an eternity for me to understand that forgiving was about shifting my perception of things.

Now, I know that forgiveness never involves passing judgement on another. It's about me, only me.

It's about me no longer thinking of myself from the point of view of how I was seen and treated by a man.

It's about me having the faith to begin again.

It's about me believing I can make the right choices for myself.

It's about me discovering my potential.

It's about me finding my path.

It's about me celebrating this life I was given.

16-year-old concluded, *I was never enough for Tony; that's just how it is. He was never in my life to bring me love. His role was to help me transform.*

Addressing me, 16-year-old said:

I'm truly sorry it took me so long to get here.

I see now that my life experience isn't about Tony or anyone else loving me; it's about me loving myself.

Ladies, she said in a confident voice, her gaze sweeping over our faces,

what I - 16-year-old - bring to the table is LOVE. The purity with which a 16-year-old loves is full of brilliance. I carry the energy of that radiant love and always will. It defines me.

I realized that the best way for me to put forgiveness into action is to focus this pure, luminous love energy into something constructive. To find that "something" I looked at my character traits. I'm a romantic, an artist at heart. As such, I believe that the best way for me to channel my love energy is through creativity.

As you are my witness, she declared in a solemn tone, *from today onward, I promise to dedicate my life to my creativity, discovering all the ways in which it can manifest itself. To begin, I'm taking up painting.*

We were all so moved we couldn't speak.

Lana and Lapis were over the moon and beaming with pride. Their 16-year-old had grown up. They decided to throw a party to celebrate the momentous event. The party was one for the books. Tables overflowed with our favorite foods; the desert table was downright decadent. There were flowers everywhere, balloons floating, music blasting. We gave 16-year-old the bumps. And, to finish with a bang, we (even Lapis) danced like it was going out of style.

16-year-old got organized. She purchased all the materials she needed and started painting. To everyone's astonishment, she was great at it. The enlightened 16-year-old found self-love and her creativity bloomed.

Well, exclaimed Lapis, *would you look at that!*
We have an artist in the family.

Chapter 15: My Body

A friend who is a professional nutritionist once told me that the human body performs best when it is slightly underweight. I was in my twenties at the time, and ever since, that has been my objective for my body.

Another uphill battle!

We come into this life with one body and, that's it. We can't trade it in for another model. I don't know about other people, but to a great extent I define myself by my body. For most of my life, what my body reflected back to me was negative: as a child, I believed my body was soiled; as an adolescent I thought I was ugly, as a young woman I felt inadequate; as a middle-aged woman I detested my body because it had become fat.

As a child I was underweight until we moved to New York City. There, our lifestyle and diet changed. There was no more romping around a big yard all day long; we lived a sedentary apartment life. Although we continued eating Haitian food, our diet didn't include the fresh fruits and vegetables we'd enjoyed in Haiti because we were poor and we ate much more bread. I went from underweight to slim, a change that wasn't noticeable enough for people around me to comment, so it didn't attract my attention.

When I got married, I began taking "the pill." It made me gain about ten pounds. Family and friends noticed and commented on the fact that I had put on weight. For the first time, I became sensitive to the issue of body weight, but it remained stable until I became pregnant.

During the first pregnancy I gained 30 pounds. Despite the fact that I breastfed for several months, I only lost ten pounds. As soon as I stopped breastfeeding, I started dieting and exercising. With extreme effort, I managed to reach 130 pounds. With my second pregnancy I again put on 30 pounds, and again, as soon as I stopped breastfeeding, I started dieting and exercising.

To control my weight, I was on a permanent diet between the ages of twenty-five and forty. Most nights, I went to bed hungry which made me feel sorry for myself. It took that much effort to keep my weight at around 130 pounds.

During the last five years of my marriage, I put on another 15 pounds which, no matter what I tried, I could not shed. Five years later, after my bright idea of getting back with Tony, I put on an extra 15 pounds during the few months that lapse of judgement lasted.

Here I was at forty-five weighing 160 pounds! It was very depressing.

Of all the things that dragged me down in my life, being overweight enraged me the most. This affliction was difficult to address because my body refused to cooperate. It's one thing for another person to act thoughtlessly toward you, but what do you do when your own body scorns you; when it seems hell bent on sabotaging your efforts to lose weight?

Being overweight made me feel as if my own body hated me. Only a person who has struggled with weight issues understands how difficult it is. Only a person who has seriously dieted understands the physical effort, the self-denial and the will it takes. I resented being fat because I was very careful about what I ate and how I treated my body in general.

The issue of body weight baffles me. Is there an animal in nature that isn't constantly eating? Their minds are on food as soon as they wake up, and they don't have weight issues! They don't have to curb their eating to remain slim. Some of us never struggle with our weight and can eat to our heart's content without ever putting on a pound. Others, like me, have to spend a significant part of our life doing what is necessary to maintain our optimum weight. Why? Why are some humans afflicted by such a calamity?

I haven't heard a single specialist say anything worthwhile on the subject of weight control. Blaming genetics, a deficit in this or that mineral or vitamin, the excess or lack of this or that gut bacteria is for the birds, in my opinion.

As usual, I had made a list of personal issues to address. Losing weight and keeping it off was at the top of my list. To control my weight, I ate "normally" five percent of the time, on special occasions such as birthdays, or family and friend get-togethers. The remainder of the time, I was an ascetic, constantly depriving myself of the foods I liked, even in the tiniest quantities. Did it make a difference? Not a big one!

What is most unfair about the weight management is that, whatever you do, it's never enough. For example, I cut sugar from my diet, eliminating foods and drinks that contain sugar. As a result, I lost a bit of weight, but then plateaued. To lose more weight I had to give up something else; this time all starches. Again, I lost a bit of weight. Considering all the foods I stopped eating by eliminating sugar and starch, the weight I lost was insignificant. The few pounds I dropped were disproportionate to the deprivation involved.

Based on my experience, the rules regarding weight loss are:

- Weight loss is never permanent;
- to maintain weight loss, you must eliminate certain foods from your diet and scale down your eating habits for life;
- if you want to lose more weight, you must eliminate more foods and scale down your eating habits significantly further, permanently; and
- there is an embedded control mechanism to keep you tightly in line: consuming any of the eliminated foods, even in very small quantity, only once, your body will immediately react and disproportionately gain weight the very next day.

How is that rational or fair?

To illustrate how the system works, I like to use the image of a ceiling. Let's imagine my eating habits and I live under a ceiling. Every time I restrict something from my diet in order to lose weight, the ceiling lowers. To lose more weight I have to lower the ceiling further, much further. If I ever eat something that belongs in the space above the level of the ceiling my body will react violently – it will have something akin to an allergic reaction because eating that particular food is no longer allowed. To become slim, I had to live under a ceiling that was two inches above the ground.

Since my mid-forties, I've had to eat fewer than one thousand calories a day to maintain my weight - most days I've lived on eight hundred calories. If I crossed the one thousand calorie ceiling, even minimally, the scale showed that I'd put on one or two pounds the following morning, without fail. I've been known to put on nine pounds in one weekend.

Clearly, weight control was a life challenge for me. It required so much effort and monopolized so much of my focus, I figured there must be a lesson linked to it. I mean, I couldn't believe I'd be faced with such an overwhelming issue for nothing.

I mulled over the question and came to see things as follows: the fundamental fact about weight control is that it's a battle.

I prefer not to get involved in battles; I find them demoralizing and tiresome. My knee-jerk reaction to any battle is to avoid it. But, despite my aversion to battle, the issue at stake was important. I tried to understand whether, in this case, it was in my best interest to fight.

The alternative to waging the battle was remaining fat. I chose the battle, hands down! No doubt, my motivation was superficial and flaky: it was about wanting to look good; but, that's important to me. It was a choice I wanted for myself.

Despite the alluring benefits of looking good, faced with the prospect of battle, my mind tried to distract me with wallowing in a depressive "why-me?" attitude instead of confronting the challenge.

Thankfully, logic prevailed. I knew enough at this stage of my life to understand that the "why-me?" question is never valid, because, why not me? I am not a victim!

What then? Well, I had to prepare for battle.

I needed a clear understanding of why I faced this challenge with my body. It occurred to me that it might simply be that some bodies are high-maintenance. For these bodies, when it comes to weight, the "maintenance" involves very hard work. With a high-maintenance body there is no day off; no time out, for life.

For whatever reason, I happen to have a high-maintenance body. That's just how it is. It's a fact of my life. I had learned acceptance of my life's circumstances. This was just one more area where it applied.

To be fully prepared, I also needed to grasp the purpose of the battle and be clear on what constituted a "win." The answer came easily. The fundamental purpose was to feel good in my skin. The "win" was having a body that could perform at its peak – a body slightly underweight.

In light of these ideas, I engaged in battle.

Anyone who has fought against weight gain knows that the body is a strong adversary. Moreover, it fights dirty. You cheat once and eat a slice of cake that weighs a quarter of a pound, and the next morning the scale shows you've put on two pounds. It will take two weeks of military-level effort to lose these two pounds. If that isn't dirty, I don't know what is!

Given the deviousness of the force I opposed, I realized that I faced a war of attrition. Regardless, I engaged. I fought this body battle tooth and nail; it took more than twenty years, but I won.

Losing the weight was excruciatingly difficult. I would lose ten pounds but then gain it back in a flash. All it took was two meals. The rigour I had to impose on myself to lose the weight was downright violent.

Looking back, I realize that the years of struggle it took to shed the weight was in reality the time it took me to walk my path of atonement. The weight loss and the transformation it produced in my body was the physical manifestation of the forgiveness; forgiveness of my sins: self-loathing, cowardice, and being a doormat. I changed those things about myself.

For more than twenty years, except on rare occasions, I refrained from eating the ice cream, the rice & beans, croissants and pizzas that others could. I stood steadfast by my choice. However, eating and sharing a meal is central to our cultures. Our civilization equates eating and sharing a meal with joy. Despite my dedication to changing my body and myself, I experienced not eating the same foods as everyone else and not sharing meals as a major hardship for more than two decades.

It was a hardship until one day my perception shifted. Pondering this lesson, I realized opting to eat differently from the people around me was simply about me, not about the people around me. Eating the way I did was about me doing right by my body. It was about me accepting and embracing my body, its needs and my choices.

I chose to do the best I can by my body. I am proud of that choice; it's a happy choice. It brought me a feeling of well-being. My reality changed completely from the day I associated my eating habits with well-being. I am a person who chooses to provide high-level maintenance care to her body and I like it.

When, some twenty years earlier I realized that wallowing in the "why-me?" attitude was a trick of the mind, what I overlooked was that the "battle" rationale had been an even bigger mind trick. My mind deceived me by making me believe that selecting what I chose to eat equated to "battle." It was a clever variation on the "why-me?" theme and I fell for it. By curbing what I ate I wasn't battling; I wasn't being crushed under a ceiling. I had been blindsided by my mind.

Another way to understand this was to experience controlling what I eat as an act of self love.

By controlling what I ate I was treating my body with respect and honor. Treating my body with reverence stemmed from self love. Self love always comes at a very high price; it requires effort, perseverance and endurance. Through sustained discipline I gave to my body the gift of thriving; it now functions in the best of conditions.

My road to slimness was arduous but, the time was not wasted because, in the end, I learned the lesson: it was about self love.

In exchange for the self-love with which I shower my body, I now have a body that performs at its peak. For the first time in my life, I love my body. I love it to the point that, at seventy years of age, I feel confident.

Chapter 16: God

I choose to be a joyful person.

A few years ago, in one of his TV shows, Gregg Braden said that our relationship with our parents defines our relationship with God. I fell off my chair! "What? No, no, no, no, no, ... I love God, truly! How can you compare and equate how I feel toward my parents to my relationship with God?"

After overcoming my initial shock and a knee-jerk reaction of denial, I gave serious thought to Mr. Braden's ideas, and it occurred to me that it's probably not possible to have a constructive relationship with God when your heart is full of judgement, resentment and fear. I decided I wanted a loving relationship with God rather than wasting the rest of my life living alienated from Him.

In order to connect with God, I knew I had to do a major clean-up inside my heart, so I lined up cleaning cloths, scrubbing brush, broom, mop, cleaning products, tied my hair back, and went to work.

"For a change," I made a list. It included the major disappointments I had faced, with the names of the people involved. My father and mother topped the list.

My father's dominant personality trait was being uncommunicative. Mostly, he kept his thoughts and feelings to himself. The only conflict I ever experienced with him was when he told me to break things off with Tony. Until then, there had never been so much as a negative ripple between us.

As is common in Haitian men, he believed that child-rearing was a mother's job, particularly for female children. When I was little, my father never took care of me physically; he never fed me, bathed me, dressed me or rocked me to sleep in his arms while singing lullaby. Moreover, he didn't engage in helping me learn how to read or count. His way of caring of his children was to be the best provider he could; everything else was a woman's responsibility.

I have no doubt he loved me dearly. Allowing me to stay quietly in a corner of his tile shop to observe the work was his way of expressing his affection. Our exchanges were telegraphic involving one or two short statements or questions, at most.

At the age of three I could read him like a book. Because he was not expansive, I learned early to pick up on subtle changes in his expression and body language. For the most part, a nuanced facial expression was all that was needed for us to communicate. We were very attuned to each other.

During the eighteen years we shared a life, not once did we have a detailed conversation on any topic. Not once did he ask me how I felt about anything. It would have involved words, and he had none. He was sensitive to my mood and, if he suspected I was sad or hurt, he would smile shyly and give me a soft pat on the head. He always steered clear of demonstrations of feeling. I can only guess at the why he had built such a thick wall around himself.

Until I was six, I was joy personified. I was very intelligent and by the time I was four my mother had taught me dozens of children's songs which I knew by heart. I didn't have a shy bone in my body and didn't need any coaxing to stand on a table and belt out my repertoire, especially if it was for my father. He loved my joyful enthusiasm and soaked it up. It energized him.

When I reached six years of age things changed; I became totally introverted. There were the traumatic abuses I've already described, and going to school was pure misery for me. Exposed to mean teachers and mean children, I became withdrawn.

As I got older and became very shy, a distance developed between my father and me. There was no tension or conflict. We weren't inclined to communicate through talking, so our exchanges were minimal. We were both quiet, but beneath our silence, a current of trust flowed.

My relationship with my mother had a totally different dynamic marked by destructive dominance and loathing toward me.

I never saw my mother genuinely smile; not once in my life. She only smirked. Depending on the circumstance, the smirk was a mechanical grin, a mocking grin, a heartless grimace, a sarcastic rictus or a sneer of disgust. Today, with the discernment of adulthood, I ask: what could have hurt her so badly that she lost the capacity to smile? Whatever it was, it had cut through her bones and slashed her spirit, probably at a very young age.

After my mother died, I learned from my siblings that she had a Multiple Personality Disorder. They only became aware of it when they themselves became adults. But by then, it was too late. Like a violent tornado, her illness left wreckage in its wake. She had lived a difficult life and, for the most part, spread misery in the lives of those around her.

With what I've learned, I now wonder what traumatic experiences she had, maybe repeatedly, during childhood that left her fractured into irreconcilable pieces?

My mother was the youngest of seven children. Her mother died when she was two years old. Her father, who believed that bringing up children was a woman's responsibility, dumped all seven children in the lap of his two sisters when his wife passed.

My relationship with my grandfather didn't go beyond "hello". He never paid any attention to me except for once; I must have been about five and blurted out something - I don't remember what. He humiliated me so harshly in front of everyone that I remember wishing I were dead. I was so crushed by the experience that from then on, I didn't trust my voice and became quiet.

Based on what my mother, aunts and uncles shared with me growing up, my grandfather was the classic egocentric spoiled brat. He was selfish, opportunist and cold-hearted.

For example, he only married my grandmother after their third child was born. That must have been excruciatingly humiliating for a young woman living in a society as conservative and small-minded as middle-class Port-au-Prince in those days. I can only imagine the suffering she endured because of the indignity my grandfather put her through.

Life after my grandmother's death must have been very difficult for the seven children. Given that my grandfather had basically washed his hands of them, they were orphans. From that day onward, they had no parental love to support them through life. Their two aunts must have been way too overwhelmed to concern themselves with any of the children's emotional well being, never-mind doting on them.

As for the aunts themselves, their lives became a struggle to meet the basic needs of seven extra people. They weren't even married. Can you imagine the upheaval? They had never signed up for such a burden; my grandfather literally robbed them of their lives because they were "family." Or more precisely, they were his sisters and, therefore subject to his authority.

The experience must have been unmanageable for everyone involved, except my grandfather, who managed to extricate himself at his sisters' expense.

To ensure his own peace of mind after abandoning his seven children to them, he made sure to reside in another city. Later, when the children had grown up and left the aunts' "nest," my grandfather moved in with them. They hadn't done enough; now that he was getting old, they had to take care of him, again, in the name of "family."

I never heard my mother or any of my aunts and uncles express a single word of gratitude toward the two aunts who had assumed their care and custody. From what I recall, they all resented these aunts for various reasons.

Appreciation, kindness, insight and understanding didn't flow in my family. The record shows that I come from a line of emotionally unavailable people.

Looking back, the day my father told me to break up with Tony, he probably believed he was doing me a favor. No doubt it hadn't taken much for him to conclude that Tony was a loser. Being a withdrawn type, he couldn't find the words that might have helped me see Tony in a different light. He cut to the chase and did what he thought was best. As Lapis would say. "In life, some things are written; they must happen; there is no escaping."

As for my mother, I cannot pinpoint the aspects of my personality that triggered her but, clearly, who I was and how I behaved emotionally set her off on many levels. For example, on the matter of sexual abuse, she probably suspected what was happening to me. Now that I understand her better, I see how that suspicion must have shattered and ravaged her with fear – the fear of having to face an annihilating pain. Blocking-out the evidence had been a survival mechanism. I had concluded she didn't love me. I was so, so wrong.

Having gone through my list, I asked myself: where does all this leave me? For one thing, I was cured of the need to ask "why?" when it involves the behavior of others. Each of us is a mystery. We have reasons for behaving as we do; sometimes we grow into understanding and sometimes we don't.

My current focus in life is on being what I want to be.

Reflecting recently about who I am, I had the following insights:

I now know myself well enough to recognize three main character traits:

- I am organized and I have a practical mind.
- I am a nurturing person, the "mother-hen" type.
- I am creative.

All of us, in trying to find and develop our true identity must work within our environment. In my case, life confronted me mostly with people - parents, siblings, husband, family, co-workers and friends - who clashed with my main character traits.

My practical and efficient mind clashed with the "idealists" who surrounded me and shared my life. They perceived my down-to-earth logic as "small-mindedness." When, for example, I made what I thought were sound economic decisions, I was compared to a donkey too stupid to realize it's chasing a carrot which is actually dangling from a stick attached to its back. Another person used the image of a hamster spinning its wheel to illustrate how they saw me: someone stuck on the money treadmill.

My "mother-hen-nurturing-the-ones-I-love" trait clashed with the "freedom seekers" in my life. They perceived my desire to take care of them as a need to control them, to clip their wings. I was told I am overbearing, that I stifle those around me, and that my tendency to nurture was just a covert way to live out the fact that I'm emotionally "needy."

My creativity, expressed in the ease at finding constructive solutions and making effortless decisions in my everyday life, has been perceived as demeaning, acting superior, or a way to put others down.

In my younger years, I was hurt, often deeply, by the criticisms of those around me, which greatly affected my perception of myself. Despite feeling crushed, I would pick myself up and go on.

With time, I realized that my drive to get back up was fueled by my resentment that others could not see me in a positive light. I spent years putting myself through unnecessary misery by asking myself "why?"

I slowly came to realize that the criticisms of those around me were nothing more than reflections of my own doubts and regrets about myself.

As the years have passed, resentment has been replaced by humility: the ability to accept that what my critics saw in me is their truth and I have to accept that without needing to understand why. Why my behavior affected them is true for them, regardless of my intentions.

Finally, at this stage of my life, I see that all these human interactions forced me to choose, every step of the way, whether I would define who I am by the opinions of others or by knowing and being myself.

Reviewing my life's past, I see that, despite many setbacks, I chose in the end to look inward to find my true identity instead of molding myself to the image others reflected back to me.

Today I celebrate that I am an organized, efficient, practical-minded person who loves to take care of and protect those I love, and who is blessed with a pinch of creativity.

I lead a very quiet life and try my best not to affect others negatively. I am the keeper solely of myself and my own heart. I try to understand and do what feels right for me. I focus on learning how to love myself.

I've made peace with my parents. They now play an active role in my life every day and show me all the ways to love Life.

After all the tidying, sweeping, washing and scouring I realize I have made only a small dent in the cleaning process. However, I am hopeful, because I believe I have cleared space that allows me to communicate with God through an opening the size of a pin-hole. My strongest desire in this lifetime is to experience communicating with God through a tiny keyhole.

I strive every day to be joyful.

Chapter 17: Sacred Places

What interests me most at this stage of my life is travelling the world to discover and experience Sacred Places.

I love pilgrimages. I am drawn to the mysterious energy of the sacred sites they lead to. Every time I expose myself to the magical powers of sacred sites, I receive special favors whose purifying energies infuse me with insights and help me better interpret my own life.

For the rest of my life, I will strive for enough harmony of body, mind and soul to find more opportunities for life-altering pilgrimages. To date, I've done several, and each has transformed me.

The following are notes from my journey to one of the most sacred sites of Tibet.

One day, while house cleaning and half-listening to a TV documentary, I heard the narrator mention a sacred lake in Asia whose waters are believed to wash away the sins of a lifetime. When I ran to the TV, I was too late to catch the name of the lake, but the small bit of information I heard had resonated deeply with me.

I researched sacred lakes and came across Lake Manasarovar; I immediately knew it was the lake I was looking for. What I read about it, and subsequently Mount Kailash, called to me, so much that I was determined to make a pilgrimage to pray at the two holy sites.

From a very young age, I have pondered the purpose of my life, always concerned about "missing the boat" in this lifetime. I was in my sixties, and generally satisfied with my life to that point, but felt an urge to expand my soul. I prayed regularly to learn how to grow fully and discern the best path for the remainder of my life.

Mount Kailash and Lake Manasarovar are two of the sacred sites most venerated by Tibetans. I undertook my pilgrimage with the intention that visiting them would touch my heart and open it to the fullest. I believed in their power. In preparation for the journey, I prayed asking for inspiration, insight and guidance on my path.

The tour I joined included a walk around Mount Kailash and a stop at Lake Manasarovar. It was gloriously beautiful on the morning we set out to walk around the mountain, the atmosphere filled with the crisp, chill air of early autumn. The emblematic snow-capped pyramid atop the southern face shone brilliantly against the limpid sapphire blue sky.

The weather was just as beautiful when we stopped at Lake Manasarovar. Offset by the violet backdrop of distant mountain ridges, from shore to shore the lake was a darker shade of steel blue and, despite a strong wind, its waters were very calm. There was a thin sheet of ice along the shoreline.

I was struck by the opposing impressions which Mount Kailash and Lake Manasarovar raised in me. Mount Kailash is an impressive 6,638 m, but for some reason, seeing it in person, it did not seem high, whether I saw it from the surrounding plain or standing right at its foot. Visually, it is not imposing, except for its crowning pyramid.

I would not describe the landscape of Mount Kailash and Lake Manasarovar as stunningly beautiful or breathtaking; I have seen many more stunning places; I found the scenery barren, desolate, primal and austere, but marveled that this starkness gave an undeniable power to the landscape. Nor did I find the place peaceful; an undercurrent of energy seemed to permeate the air, a force so strong it was almost palpable. It brought me to my knees.

I was subdued by the energy; all I could do was let go. At the same time, everything about the place was imbued with an unexpected stillness that calms and opens the heart. I was overcome by deep feelings of reverence and awe.

The ritual walk around Mount Kailash proved beyond my physical capabilities. Heart and lungs reeling from the altitude, I had to turn back after 8 kilometers of the circuit.

During my walk at the foot of Mount Kailash I prayed at regular intervals, consciously opening my heart to experience the power of the place. When I knelt and prayed at the foot of the mountain, I had the distinct feeling of hearing a faint whisper; when I knelt on the shore of Lake Manasarovar and baptized myself with its waters, I registered the same whisper. At the time, the sounds were drowned by my overwhelming fatigue, but despite their elusiveness, the gentle whispers filled my consciousness and stayed with me.

After I returned home, it took several weeks to calm my mind enough to hear the whispers of Mount Kailash and Lake Manasarovar. Their message was simple: "follow your heart." As soon as I heard that, memories of the trip came flooding back.

I remembered that on the drive to Mount Kailash we passed through an area where the mountains were speckled with tufts of low, creeping vegetation. The green tufts formed interesting shapes, and my eyes began spotting heart-shaped clumps. Like a child, I looked for heart shapes on every mountain we passed. Love flooded my heart.

And I remembered that just as I turned back to the village because I could not pursue the trek around Mount Kailash, I looked down and saw a heart-shaped pebble at my feet. Again, love flooded my heart; I picked up the pebble and kissed it. I was deliriously happy to have found this beautiful little heart, ecstatic as only a child can be about such a simple thing.

The intense emotions these hearts aroused made clear that they were trying to tell me something but, at the time, I could not figure out what.

Though my body was completely exhausted from my visit to Mount Kailash and Lake Manasarovar, I left Tibet with a figurative spring in my step. I felt serene and a sense of harmony settled over me.

I now carry with me a renewed vision of my path. I understand that it's not so much about what to do with the remainder of my life but that everything I do, even the smallest decision, should honor the values I hold dear in my heart. It's about going deeper into myself to get closer to who I really am and being constantly receptive to things that delight me and make my heart smile; the rest will follow.

As for the future, soon I am going back to the pyramids of Egypt. I will spend a whole night alone in the King's Chamber of Koepp's pyramid. I have great expectations for this experience.

I am filled with life as I have never been before.

Life is good.

Chapter 18: Being in Good Company

Lana and Lapis are protective forces that come into their full power in times of trouble. By nature, they are formidable; but when I experience happiness and peace, when things are calm, which nowadays is almost always, they operate on a dialed-back energy. It's just as potent, but not intense Their vibe becomes serenely joyful and they dote on me affectionately. I am never, never alone.

They don't decide on my behalf; they respect my free will. All my choices are mine. That said, they don't always approve of my choices and don't hesitate to give me a piece of their mind. In life-or-death situations, however, they shove aside "free will" and override me, body and mind, for a few seconds.

Once, when I was about five, my father and some workers were repairing a large tile press in the shop. One of the men lost his footing and accidentally leaned on the press to get his balance; the press toppled. My back was to a wall and I stood directly in the trajectory of the falling machine. Had my instincts kicked-in, I would have tried to escape and would have been crushed because whatever I had done would have been too slow. I blacked out for a second, during which a "force" kept me frozen, plastered to the wall. The machine missed me by a hair.

Lana and Lapis are the best company; they adore me and entertain me to no end. They are intensely curious about every little thing I think or do. And they enjoy seeking new experiences with me.

Lana loves getting involved when I purchase things. At the store she stands in front of me and gets so engrossed in poring over displays that she's oblivious to the fact that she's blocking my view. Even when I tap her on the shoulder to indicate I would like to take a look too, she reluctantly takes a teeny, tiny step to the side and gives me a questioning glance that says: "oh, you want to look as well?" Her expression shows that she'd prefer to tell me to "go sit down, I'll take care of everything" and then find me the best options. Her eyes say: "I've got this, my Chérie; all you'll have to do is pick the one you prefer."

Lapis knows that I love devices designed to improve human function. She acts like an antenna, always ready to seek information on items that may please me. For example, she brought me information on pyramids. I now sleep under one every night. She drew my attention to violet-ray machines, and, I now take an electrical bath every day. Each piece of jewelry I wear was selected by Lapis for its energetic essence. I have many interesting gadgets thanks to her.

And their enthusiasm when I come up with a project like remodeling and decorating my apartment or a room! They are beside themselves with excitement. Lapis is all about functionality and budget; Lana is good at sketching and creating atmosphere. "Passionate" doesn't begin to describe their involvement; they are the reason my apartments are always so beautiful and original.

Although they are dead ringers for each other, they have distinct mannerisms. For example, when Lapis is concentrating, she lowers her eyes to the left side without turning her face, assessing the situation. Lana and I call it the "side glance." Invariably, the side-glance is followed by a brilliant idea.

By the time she directs her gaze forward again she has the answer to whatever she was contemplating. It's mystifying! Every time she does the side-glance, Lana and I figuratively like dogs, sit back on our haunches to await the treat we know is coming - what Lapis has come up with. She always has innovative ideas and piercing insight.

There was this time I experienced a difficult situation at work. A senior architect who was very insecure perceived my productivity and accomplishments as efforts to outperform him. To discredit me, he spread false information about my work. I felt overwhelmed by the situation and didn't know how to handle it. I submitted my concerns to Lapis. She did a side-glance and then said:

No matter what he does, always remain supremely indifferent to his harassment.

I followed her advice. My attitude frustrated him to distraction. He could not understand how, despite the many obstructions he created to undermine my efficiency and credibility, I never faltered, never broke a sweat, and continued to perform to my usual high standards. In the end, he left me alone.

When Lana gets excited about something, she rapidly and repeatedly snaps her index finger against the middle finger of her right hand to express her delight. It's a very Haitian gesture. Lana is so expressive!

A few years ago, I did my first important pilgrimage; the visit to Mount Kailash and Lake Manasarovar. It was an exceptional adventure and I expressed the desire to do more pilgrimages.

Lana came running, fingers snapping and grinning from ear to ear.

I've got it, I've got it,' she said, *I've got the perfect trip for you. Go to Egypt; visit the Pyramids and the Temples along the Nile.*

I did as Lana suggested, and the experience was life-altering.

Nowadays, Lana and Lapis, although still very different, are perfectly synchronized, to the point that they often finish each other's sentences. But that wasn't always the case. Before the pilgrimage with Ti-Chérie, their plans were coordinated, in the sense that they worked towards a common goal: protecting and taking care of me. But in those days, they worked separately, and sometimes their approaches didn't coincide when it came to the details.

For example, they once told me about what happened on a Caribbean Carnival Day. It occurred before Lapis felt free to express her emotions and before I met them:

The Summer Carnival parade in our part of the city, where there are many Caribbean residents, features floats with bands whose repertoire includes the latest hits and popular oldies. The public joins the parade, and people gather around their favorite band to dance, moving with the floats as the parade progresses. Every summer my best friend and I attended the parade together and danced the day away.

Lana was overjoyed at the prospect of spending the day dancing. Caribbean parade day was by far her favorite. To set the mood while getting ready, she played the music on full blast; it got into her bloodstream and called to her African origins. She was buzzing to the infectious vibe; she sang and danced, marking the beat with every step, swaying her hips and snapping her pelvis to the sensual rhythm. Her dancing was a show in itself.

For this event people didn't dress-up as for a Mardi-gras parade, so Lana chose her best-fitting jeans, a very bright T-shirt, and her most comfortable sneakers. For a festive touch, she wore strings of colourful beads around her neck and shiny bangles in her ears. Her thick curly hair was loose, and she held a whistle between her lips - a whistle is a must for carnival.

When she met up with Lapis, she stopped dead in her tracks. Lapis was wearing no-nonsense (well ironed) black pants with a white short-sleeve shirt, her every-day leather shoes and her hair tied back in a matron-like bun.

That's what you're wearing to the carnival? asked Lana astonished.

What's the problem? inquired Lapis innocently.

Today is about fun, explained Lana.

Chérie is going to the parade to have fun, to forget her troubles and let loose. How is she supposed to let loose when you are dressed as if you were going to the office? You're overdressed for church, for heaven's sake!

We're both wearing pants and a short-sleeve top, Lapis pointed out objectively.

Lana pumped the volume of the music and cranked up the bass to accentuate the pounding of the drums before asking Lapis:

How exactly did you plan to "let loose" to this music in this attire?

Letting loose" is not in my vocabulary, replied Lapis, unperturbed.

You don't say, Lana muttered sarcastically under hear breath.

So, why are you even going to the parade? asked Lana.

Someone must be on body-guard duty while others are "letting loose".

Lana stepped behind Lapis, untied her bun, combed her fingers through the riotous curls, and patted down some way ward locks of the unruly mane.

We have to support Chérie, she said in a moving tone, looking at Lapis with pleading eyes.

And how exactly is hair falling in my eyes when there is an emergency going to help me be supportive?

Lana's shoulders slumped. She sighed and dropped her head forward theatrically in defeat.

As soon as they arrived at the parade Lana began dancing wildly to help me lose myself in the music. She glanced over at Lapis, who stood impassive. She stepped closer to Lapis and asked suspiciously:

You're Vulcan, right?

Exasperated with Lapis' composure, Lana stuck the whistle she had brought between Lapis' lips.

Lapis removed the whistle from her mouth, looked at it and did a side-glance. With a blank expression that Mr. Spock himself would have envied, she said to Lana:

I'll hold the fort; you go shake "what your mama gave you" to encourage Chérie.

Since I can double-task, continued Lapis, *I'll play the whistle to uphold the carnival spirit.*

She slipped the mouthpiece between her lips and blew a combination of short and long shrill, high-pitched sounds in perfect counterpoint to the music.

Lana froze, flabbergasted by the sound of Lapis' extraordinary whistle-blowing; she elevated the plastic toy to orchestra-instrument level!

Seeing the effect of her whistle-blowing skills had on Lana, Lapis commented deadpan:

Vulcans are very musical.

Lana threw back her head in a peal of laughter.

I had a memorable time.

More recently, when things were looking much better, Lapis put forward the idea that we needed a toy.

We deserve a nice toy, she stated with conviction.

What did you have in mind? I asked with keen interest?

A Karmann Ghia, she said, with a grin and twinkling eyes.

Yes, yes, yes! I shouted with glee.

What a fantastic idea! I cheered, clapping enthusiastically.

What's a Karmann Ghia? asked Lana?

It's the ultimate "chick" car - a thing of bea-u-u-u-u-ty, said Lapis in a passionate, know-it-all tone.

Leave it with me, Lapis said to me.

I'll find our car.

And indeed, she found us the perfect Karmann Ghia. Knowing I don't drive a stick-shift, Lapis chose a semi-automatic model. I couldn't believe my luck seeing the car; she was an absolute jewel. We nicknamed her Kami.

From the first day we drove her, the car turned heads everywhere we went. Even on the highway drivers slowed down to film us with their phones. All the attention made me self-conscious.

We're really being show-offs, I said to the girls.

I feel terribly self-conscious, I confessed shyly.

Self-conscious? I'll have none of that! declared Lana.

Get behind me, girls, and do what I do – showing-off falls in my skill-set.

Under Lana's tutelage Kami brought out a side of me I didn't even know existed. I realized I have a wild streak that's a mile wide! The gut-deep happiness I experienced with Kami was an off-the-charts, awe-inspiring feeling. The moments of pure delight the three of us enjoyed with Kami are indescribable.

Kami marked a turning point in my life, an indicator that I had stepped into a new reality. Trust, joy, security, confidence, freedom, pleasure and good health became my new normal. I had found my rhythm. I had never been happier in my life. It felt like a miracle.

Not long after, other changes occurred. I was comfortably sprawled on the sofa, Lana was sitting cross-legged in an oversized armchair and Lapis was on the floor, legs extended, her back leaning against the TV stand. We were just shooting the breeze when Lana and I spotted Lapis' side-glance. We quickly sat up and took notice; our hearts flip-flopped with excitement.

Realizing she was being observed, Lapis looked up and found Lana and me agog, waiting expectantly for her to share what was percolating in her mind. A natural at initiating gutsy, ambitious ideas, Lapis gave us a warm lobsided grin and, her face alive with pleasure, said:

We're a great team, right? And life is looking up, so, how about we bump things to another level, make the best of the time we have left to live and ...

... and pack in the most experiences we can, jumped in Lana, completing Lapis' thought.

Exactly, continued Lapis, eyes dancing, *let's seek new experiences.*

We need a bold plan, supplied Lana, captivated.

How about moving...

... to another country? they blurted together eagerly, their eyes filled with the gleam of adventure and fearlessness.

The idea spoke to my intrepid heart and my newfound wild streak as if it was exactly what I had been waiting for. I did a happy dance. Giddy with joy like a little girl, my heart swelled. Flanked by Lana and Lapis, my new mantra became: "Life, here I come!"

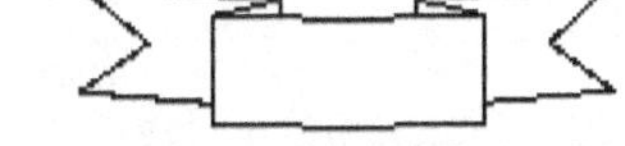

---

[1] Nick name given to François Duvalier who was president of Haiti from 1957 until his death in 1971.

www.ingramcontent.com/pod-product-compliance
Lightning Source LLC
Chambersburg PA
CBHW031414150726

47989CB00002B/660